The Weavers

Odara's Rise (Book 2 of 3)

CARLA J. LAWSON

The Weavers: Odara's Rise (Book 2 of 3)

Carla J. Lawson

© 2020

All rights reserved. No portion of this book may be reproduced, photocopied, stored, or transmitted in any form except by prior approval of the author or the publisher, except as permitted by U.S. copyright law.

Published by CJL Books &
www.diverseskillscenter.com

Editing by Rothesia Stokes

Printed in the United States of America

U.S. Copyright 1-8454541381
ISBN: 978-1-7347924-0-9

Table of Contents

Dedication

The Weavers is a fictional story that was inspired by several publications of articles about the lack of coverage for the 64,000 missing Black women in the United States of America. The articles that I came across date back as early as 2016. The sadness and hopelessness that I felt when reading about these women and girls was overwhelming.

In The Weavers, I aspired to insert hope and compassion and bring awareness into the light. The lack of media coverage and lack of outrage for these women of color whose lives and whose family's lives have been disrupted has not seemed to have changed much. In the story that I have created, I chose to fight fiercely for their recovery and survival.

This book is dedicated to the families of the missing women, the missing women themselves and to the people who actually give a damn about the existence, necessity and importance of the protection and survival of Black women.

Acknowledgements

I would like to thank the following people from the depths of my heart for their physical support and financial contributions towards the completion of this book "The Weavers", Odara's Rise book 2 of 3:
Erma Smith, Jennifer Blackman, Corey Lawson, Lillie Freightman, Flossie Weir, Michelle Prior Alameda, Raymond Deshawn Hackett, Ola lawson, Lester Jones, Regina Knight and Dwight Hilton.

Because of your contributions, this book became a reality. Your contributions allowed me to create and write in peace, without having to stress about the overhead of the publication and printing processes. I cannot express how deeply moved I am by your kindness and generosity.

I would also like to thank everyone who offered moral support and encouragement. Your contributions to my well-being and positive state of mind were just as critical to the development and completion of this project.

Last, but definitely not the least, I would like to acknowledge the people whose energies inspired characters and allowed me to use their names or the names of their children or loved ones for said characters: Lisa Mills Washington, Ola Lawson, Linda Hill Chaney, Glenda Pier Roberts, Kelly Ceballos, Apollo Ceballos, Ronnie Winbush, Jahiya Marks Garris and Watani Marks-McThomas.

Ms. Cynthia Johnson, my gratitude may never be able to equal what you pour into my spirit. Thank you for your integrity, hard work and dedication, you are greatly appreciated.

Introduction

The threads were all textures, lengths, and colors. Intisar sat at her loom, pausing to admire the new pattern that was forming. There hadn't been any new threads delivered to her lately and that meant that she could continue to let this pattern evolve. It was beautiful. Rich, vibrant, and harmonious. Much different from the previous section of the tapestry where the colors kept getting darker – some of the threads were frayed and broken off. That section was very difficult to get through. There was no rhythm to it. Just chaos and dead ends. She was absolute about who she was, and she knew what her purpose was: to continue to weave the tapestry with the threads of life throughout the world for all time, regardless of how the threads appeared.

When God would sometimes appear with a drastic change of color and texture, it was usually for balance. The patterns would become erratic, hard to follow or understand. It was at times frustrating, but it at least made for interesting conversation when they talked. He looked tired at times but always all powerful. Intisar knew that a change was coming when he would show up shaking his head and hand her random threads. He knew that she would simply get to work; intertwining them into the current pattern on the loom, even if it changed the course of what she was creating completely. Intisar never questioned him of course. I mean, he was God after all. Occasionally, she would say, "I wish this wasn't necessary." He would take a seat in the rocking chair by the window on the other side of the room where the light was always perfect, and then he would always respond with a heavy sigh and the same answer, "So do I."

And so it was, her entire existence and purpose, was to sit at this massive loom and weave a never-ending tapestry that mapped out the lives of every living, breathing being on planet Earth. Of course, this is no easy feat, despite the fact that she had come from a long lineage of master weavers and currently lived with four other women in her family who also had been called. Accepting what she had been chosen to do and actually doing it took some adjusting. That is putting it mildly, but it pales in comparison to the moment when God shows up in your home and tells you what he needs you to do – in person and in plain English. All you can do is accept that your life is no longer yours, and that it will never be the same, and then, get to it.

That is what she did. Her name is Intisar Augustin, and this is her incredible story.

Somewhere far away...

1
The Augustin House

The family consisted of six sisters, Glenda, Zora, Samara, the twins, Linda and Ola, their mother Bessie, their mother's twin sister Ethel B, and Intisar. Chronologically, it would be Intisar, Glenda, Linda and Ola, Zora and Samara. The memories Intisar has of their father Benjamin are loving but few. He worked on fishing boats and would often be gone from home for six months to a year. He would return home with a lot of money and gifts for their mother. There would be a welcome home feast, and he would take Intisar everywhere he went during his two or three-week break. Then he had to go. Her mama would cry a little, and he would hold her hand. They would stay up the entire night sitting on the porch, swinging in silence the night before he had to leave. By the time Intisar got up in the morning, he would be gone, and every other year, her mama would be pregnant again. Intisar was 14 years old when Mr. Porter showed up at the time a feast was set for her daddy to arrive and enjoy. He, Mama Bessie, and Aunt Ethel B went into the big room to have a conversation, and Intisar and her sisters sat at the table waiting patiently, wondering why he was there, and their daddy wasn't. They rarely had guests, so they assumed he would probably be joining them. Intisar's sisters were chattering and singing nursery rhymes when she heard a loud thud. She slid from her chair and ran into the big room. Her mama was on the floor in Aunt Ethel B's arms, and Mr. Porter – who was a big strong man, was holding up Aunt Ethel B with one arm and fanning her mama's head with the other. Tears were in his eyes, and Intisar knew instantly that her daddy wasn't coming home this time. Mr. Porter had come to tell her mama that the boat her daddy left on had gotten swept out to deep sea during a bad storm and never came back. As Mr. Porter and Aunt Ethel B helped her mama into her bedroom, Intisar was instructed to bring a pitcher of water to the room and fix the dinner plates for her sisters. She moved quickly and without question.

When Intisar returned to the dining room to serve her sisters their dinner, there was an eerie silence. All the chattering and singing had stopped. They all had their heads down while she was preparing plates – except for Samara, the youngest of her siblings, the most precocious, the most energetic, and the one that Aunt Ethel B said was "gifted." Samara saw the sadness in her eyes, and she got up and put her little six-year-old arms around Intisar's waist and said, "It'll be alright. We'll be fine. We just have to love Mama more now." Intisar kissed her on her forehead and told her to sit down so they could bless the table and eat. Many things ran through her mind during that meal. Intisar realized and understood that she would never see her daddy again while processing that she had only seen him for two weeks at a time, twice a year, every year of her life. Intisar was doing the math. She couldn't taste her food, her heart was beating slowly, and she could hear it in her head. In her entire life, Intisar had only spent fourteen months with her daddy. One year and two months, and now he was gone. She swallowed it all with her dinner. Somewhere between the lemonade she drank after eating her meal and the peach cobbler she served to her siblings for dessert, Intisar heard him say goodbye. At the exact moment that she heard his voice and smiled, her baby sister Samara looked up at her and said, "I told you."

In less than a month after they found out that their daddy had died, the house returned to normal. At least normal for them, since their lives were far from that – they just didn't know it. Intisar's mother and Aunt Ethel B were master weavers, and anyone born into their family was introduced to weaving as soon as they were tall enough to sit at a loom. Mama Bessie had a workshop adjacent to the house that had several small rooms in it. Each room held a small table, a lamp, and a loom. A prayer closet was located in the front of the workshop. For her entire life, there would always be someone in it. Intisar's mama took turns with Aunt Ethel B. While one was praying, the other would be working, and after a few hours, they would switch. The sisters saw them together at the same time only for Sunday dinners. Whoever was not in the closet was the one who had charge over the children. It was a flawless system of respect and accountability. Intisar and her sisters, as children didn't know life to be any other way.

In the mornings, their breakfast was always ready before they woke up. They ate together, and the children who were old enough to weave automatically headed to the workshop and began their day of work. No one ever asked what they were making, who it was for, or why they had to do it. They just did it. Their mama told them that they were a "chosen" people. That they served a mighty purpose and sooner or later, it would be revealed to them what that meant. She made mention from time to time of a "visit" that would make it all make sense, and in the meantime, they needed to just do the work. So, they did. Every one of them had the gift. As the years passed, they became master weavers themselves, all six of them, and they learned one by one why they were weaving, and for whom they were weaving. Their lives became almost magical.

Looking back, Intisar realized that they always had more than enough of everything. Even after her daddy died, food and the necessities of life were plentiful. It never occurred to her that her mama or Aunt Ethel B never left the house to go to work nor did anyone else. Because of the structure of their lives, she also never took note that only once or twice a year did someone come visit. When people did visit, the basic niceties were exchanged and some type of hors d'oeuvres were served. After an hour or so, they usually ended up purchasing one of the many tapestries that hung on the walls of the big room, and then they were gone.

When company came, they all stopped what they were working on and joined their mama or Aunt Ethel B to entertain them. Glenda was usually asked to sing a few bars of someone's favorite spiritual. The twins, Linda and Ola, would show their latest tapestry creations. Zora would tell a short story or anecdote and Samara would usually offer some sort of spiritual advice or direction, based on the flow of the conversation and whatever energies she picked up on from their guests. Intisar would play the piano or engage in a game of chess or checkers. Visitors were always pleasant and appreciative of their hospitality. Before leaving, they would always compliment Mama Bessie or Aunt Ethel B on their social graces and beauty and sometimes ask if they had any potential suitors. There was never an answer provided for that question. Just a sincere thank you and acknowledgment of the compliments as visitors were escorted to the front door. Once they were gone, everyone did whatever was necessary to return the big room to its original state. They would then return to the workshop to continue weaving in their personal rooms for working, which by the way, none of them ever entered unless it was their own room.

From the outside of the Augustin home, any onlooker would have seen a small plantation style home sitting in the middle of a couple of very well-manicured acres. Upon a closer look, they would have even noticed a second small cottage adjacent to the main house. They didn't have any farm animals but plenty of fresh growing vegetables and a few fruit trees. A few benches sporadically placed in the shade under the fruit trees provided ambiance and a place to rest outdoors. Intisar's favorite bench sat under the Magnolia tree behind the main house. It was all quite appealing aesthetically, the whole view of it all, and it was designed to be so. What you saw on the outside, however, is by far not what you would have seen had you been welcomed inside – especially inside of the workshop.

At 5 a.m. every morning, no matter where they were on their property, or what they were doing, everyone stopped to have tea together. That tea was the only thing they put into their bodies during the week until Sunday dinner, when they all dined together. Whoever was not in the prayer closet between Mama Bessie and Aunt Ethel B also joined them. During their teatime, Intisar and her sisters would have conversations about how amazed they were with one another and they doted very heavily on each other for the next half an hour. If one or any of them was working on something that was disturbing, all the others sat closely to that sister and almost surrounded her so that she felt comforted and supported. They would stay there in silence during those times, allowing whoever needed love and empathy to soak up as much as they could before the day began, and the pain that sometimes needed to be endured while creating resumed its space. If you're wondering what they all did, it's quite simple and incredibly elaborate at the same time. Intisar's mother

Bessie, her mother's twin sister Aunt Ethel B, all five of her sisters, and Intisar, had the task of recording the lives and journeys of everyone in every dimension of the universe by weaving their stories onto massive, sometimes seemingly never-ending tapestries. They were all visited by God at different intervals in their lives and instructed about what they were to do. Simply put, God showed up, told them why He created them, and what they were to do for the rest of their lives. He would then visit them from time to time to bring them the threads of life for them to use.

When God appeared to Intisar, it was always in a very attractive, gentle male form. He had a sense of humor and usually sat for a while after handing her the threads that she was to use. Glenda saw an older male, strong in build and aggressive in spirit. The twins, Linda and Ola, didn't see a personification – they saw the light and heard their instructions, and their threads appeared on huge spindles. Zora didn't see or hear anything. She just looked up and her threads were neatly bound and placed in the basket next to her loom. The only interaction she had was a gentle breeze that made her smile. The youngest sister Samara saw an incredibly beautiful and strong looking woman. Sometimes Black, sometimes Indian, sometimes

Hispanic, but always with great beauty and power. Her visits from God were usually the longest. Why? Because she was Samara and she had questions. Also, because she was empathic and had the gift of sight. God was constantly downloading and preparing her for what she was about to feel or see so that she could work undistracted and not be troubled by anything when her threads got darker and screamed out in pain. Intisar's mama and Aunt Ethel B only had one interaction with God and that was when they were called at the same time to do this work. They were informed that all their offspring would be called to do the same work, and that they would never have to worry about how to survive. They were instructed to pray in shifts until their last breaths and never question the changes that would go on around them to make their home more comfortable and their days easier. After that, their threads would appear simultaneously, hanging in large skeins on the walls of the rooms that they worked in. Intisar's mama and Aunt Ethel B never saw God again, nor heard God's voice. They just felt everything. Deeply and intensely, they felt everything that was being woven by all of the sisters, and they did it without one word of question or complaint. They felt it all and submitted to prayer without wavering. They began to become like one well-oiled machine; moving like clockwork, doing what God had assigned, from sunup to sundown, every single day.

2
Odara's New Home

Odara sat perfectly still with her mind on a million things while the artist painted her picture. She was sitting in a field of wildflowers on a blanket, wearing a beautiful embroidered gold gown, exquisite jewelry, and a large white flower in her hair. The background of the flowers in the field and the sun against her dark chocolate skin made for an incredibly stunning portrait. She had no idea why she was in southern France, obviously during renaissance, or what assignment was in store for her. As usual, the Sacred Council had simply reassigned her with no instruction or information. The best part was that she was able to remain in the body of Odara, a physical embodiment that she had grown to love. There had been many times before when she was sent as a warrior from the spiritual realm, where the body that she had chosen to occupy for her earthly assignment expired before she was reassigned. But not this time. She was still Odara, and as a result of her last assignment, she was stronger and wiser.

The artist painting her portrait was a young man with a strong build and a very serious face and demeanor. While wondering how to breach conversation with him, she heard his name in the wind. After Odara gave a silent thanks for that small gift, the artist spoke, "I am finished, Mademoiselle. I hope that you will be pleased. It has been an honor for you to allow me the pleasure of capturing your beauty. Please tell me what you think." He turned the canvas around and helped her to her feet. Odara stood with his assistance, smoothed out her gown, and then looked up to see the painting. She swooned at the sight of it. Seeing her image perfectly replicated on canvas with all the flowers and incredible colors that he brought to life moved her intensely. Speechless, a single tear fell from the corner of her eye. The painting was incredible. She put her hand over her heart and when it contacted the broach she was wearing, the information she needed for this conversation downloaded into her spirit. The broach was a gift from Amaterasu of the Sacred Council – a beautiful jeweled Sun, and she hadn't realized until then that she was wearing it. Giving silent thanks again, she listened to the information and then turned to face the artist. "Randall, this is incredible work. I absolutely love it! I must increase your commission! I knew when I first saw you painting in town on the street to make extra money that you were gifted, but this — this is beyond words. No more street corners for you, Sir! I'm going to see to it." Randall was humbled by her praise. He smiled and graciously accepted her compliments and told her that when the painting was completely dry, he would deliver it to her. He began to pack everything into her carriage and helped her into it. As they rode back to town, he sat across from her, admiring her beauty and the undercurrent of strength that made her quite alluring. They made small talk and enjoyed the ride, but there was something slightly puzzling to him. He never remembered anyone living in the house that she occupied and hadn't seen anyone Black of her means in his town before. *Who was she? What does she do and why was she here?* he ponders. None the less, it didn't matter. A commission like this would make a huge difference for his family, and the word would get out that HE painted that portrait. Randall was looking forward to a new level of respect and pay as an artist.

The carriage arrived at Odara's chateau, and she sat in amazement looking at it through the carriage window. She had asked jokingly to be rich for her next assignment and the Sacred Council had most definitely honored her request. The grounds were beautiful, well-manicured, and vibrant red, purple, orange, and pink flowers graced the entire walkway to the front door. She took a deep breath and tried to contain her excitement. While the spirit in her was only focused on what her assignment would be, the human part of Odara was ready to see just how well she was going to be living for this time period.

She walked slowly from the carriage to the house. Taking in the beauty of the front grounds, Odara took the time to survey every inch of her surroundings. Taking note that the purple orchids near the front door swayed in acknowledgement of her presence as she passed them, she was caught off guard when the front door opened. A very striking caramel-colored woman greeted her with, "Welcome home, Mademoiselle Odara." Odara smiled and said, "Thank you, it's been a long journey." Giselle, the woman who opened the door, took Odara's shawl and informed her that lunch was already prepared, and she just needed to know if it should be served in the dining room, the garden, or on the patio. Tickled by the formality of it all, Odara told her she wanted to be served on the patio in thirty minutes because she wanted to change clothes. Giselle responded with a bow and a "Very well, Ma'am," before heading down a hallway graced with beautiful artwork and tapestries.

Odara was clueless about the layout of her own home, and there seemed to be quite a few rooms. She remembered the broach and placed her hand over it while looking around at the sculptures in the entryway. Instantly receiving a flood of information about her home, the city, and her staff, she felt the broach go cold. Grateful for the information that she could now use to move ahead until she was face to face with her new assignment, she headed up the spiral staircase that led to her bedroom.

The master bedroom was the last room at the end of the hallway. As she passed each of the other rooms, she looked inside of them. Uniquely decorated, there was a sitting room, another bedroom, a library, a dressing room, and then her bedroom. The hallway itself was quite spectacular. Marble floors with inlaid mosaics sporadically placed. Floor to ceiling drapes and tapestries. Artwork and mirrors with hand carved frames, and the most perfect purple and turquoise velvet-tufted benches, in between every other room, on both sides of the hallway. Every room seemed to have its own individual theme. In every room there was at least one item from her previous home that had modified itself to fit into the style and time of its surroundings.

Odara noted the Spirit Lock on the dressing room door. That lock which could only be seen by her, could also only be opened by her. The dressing room held the chest that the Sacred Council randomly placed gifts in for her as well as the hidden pantry, that in more modern times, was usually located in the kitchen. She found that to be interesting and couldn't wait for the pantry to call out for her presence. The scent of fresh lavender came to her, courtesy of a breeze. She was at the doorway to her bedroom and the scent that brought her back to focus was coming from that room. Odara knew that being able to smell the lavender meant one very important thing—her garden had been safely transferred AND it had to be adjacent to her boudoir. Perfect.

She opened the door to the master suite and stood inhumanly, still taking in the layout and design. Incredibly elegant in every way, the bedroom was a myriad of her favorite colors and textures. Purple, gold, fuchsia, orange, turquoise, red, white, and emerald green. The colors were perfectly balanced throughout with silk and velvet pillows, throws, wall tapestries, throw rugs, and draperies. The main furniture pieces were white with gold trim, and they were of the finest craftsmanship. More breathtaking than the room being alive with color were the windows that went from floor to ceiling on each side of the room. They were strategically placed so that if you were lying in bed, you could watch the sun rise on one side and see it set on the other. She walked to the French doors adjacent to the closet and saw that there was a balcony with full patio seating. Opening the doors, the scent of fresh lavender, now stronger, came floating into the room. Looking down over the balcony, Odara saw that her garden was almost completely transferred from her last home. The garden acknowledged her presence by emitting the various scents that some of the plants and herbs were known for. She spoke into the wind, "Welcome, thank you for joining me for another season of life." She turned and went back into the bedroom. Sitting down on a white overstuffed sofa, she took a deep breath and began to center herself. The Sacred Council had really honored her request for an assignment where she would be rich. As much as physical accoutrements meant nothing to them, they had placed her in a life of luxury for this part of her journey as a warrior.

The Sacred Council consisted of powerful deities from several different cultures around the world. They all held the ability to change the course of the world as we knew it when they worked together for the greater good of the universe. To be a part of the council, they all had to agree to assimilate the spirit warriors from their various cultures into one giant force. With each of them having their own gifts and strengths that made them the most powerful of their own regions, together with the warriors that chose to help keep order in the universe – they were an unstoppable force. The Sacred Council consisted of: Isis, an Egyptian Goddess with magical powers greater than all other Egyptian Gods. She also held power over fate itself; Shango, Yoruba God of thunder, lightning, and justice; Oya, one of the most powerful Orishas and the wife/sister of Shango, Goddess of the winds, lightning, violent storms, death and rebirth; Kali, Hindu Goddess of time and change and destroyer of evil forces; Amaterasu, Japanese Goddess of the Sun and universe; The Holy Trinity, the Father, the Son (Jesus), and the Holy Spirit, the triune God of Christian faith and unconditional love; Bitol, Mayan sky God who participated in the last two attempts at creating humanity. The combination of these deities and the spirit warriors they pulled together to help maintain the balance of good had been successful for longer than time had been recorded. She thought about what an honor it was to be chosen to serve them and then shifted her thoughts to clarification of her current situation.

After a few minutes of meditating, she was able to focus on her reality. Regardless of this beautiful home, the obviously affluent lifestyle that she had been given, along with a plethora of aesthetically pleasing accoutrements, she was here on assignment. The physical surroundings were just fluff for the comfort of her physical body; she was not to get caught up on the physicality of any of it. Created through fire and given the name Machaneka, currently in the body of Odara, she was a spiritual warrior who fought for the greater good of the universe.

There were to be no distractions due to lavish belongings and environments. "Now, get it together!" she said aloud to herself. "You are only residing in this body to do the work you were called to do." That reminded her that she was supposed to go downstairs for a meal in thirty minutes. She got up and went to the closet to find something light and comfortable to change into. The closet was full of brightly colored lounge wear and robes. She reached for a royal blue pant set and noticed some folded fabrics on a shelf. Grabbing the fabrics and the set, she took off the full-length gown that she was wearing and instantly felt free.

Unfortunately, in a house with a full staff of servants, walking around naked wasn't an option, so she slid into the pant set and was thankful that fabric was not only light, but soft and soothing. She laid the dress on her bed and sat down to look at the fabrics. She unfolded them and spread them out on the floor. They were tapestries of the finest workmanship that she had ever seen. Beautiful beyond words, and they were folded up in the closet like spare blankets. She looked up and saw something that she didn't notice when she first walked into the room, a large portrait, no, a picture of an angel.

Dark skinned, well-defined body, several sets of wings, a beautiful smile, and eyes that looked like… "Jerod!" she screamed his name. Taking a deep breath, Odara remembered the last time she saw him when he helped to take care of her after a brutal attack. She heard the ruffle of feathers and smiled. He said he would always be near. He was keeping his word. Looking back at the fabric on the floor, she noticed what looked like a couple of small moth holes in each of them. Running her hands across the fabric where the holes were, she felt the sensation of heat in her hands. Thinking that there couldn't be a significance to the fabric, she ran her hands over the rest of it. Nothing. She traced the holes again with her fingers and the heat began to fill her palms. Then she felt a sense of nausea as several strong emotions coursed through her body, amongst them were dread and sadness. Stepping back and standing over the tapestries, she folded them and gathered them up.

Odara went to her dressing room door with the tapestries in hand and addressed the Spirit Lock. With one palm placed directly in the center of the door, she spoke, "Alatradias, Pasnida damelecha salimnious." The sound of several locks opening quickly graced the hallway. She then turned the knob and opened the door. Once inside, she faced the doorway and saw the new lock passwords formulate. She memorized them and closed the door. She carried the tapestries over to the cedar chest that had been created by a master craftsman who created specifically for the Sacred Council. The chest, now almost full after centuries of gifts from the Sacred Council, always revealed what she needed for an assignment if there was impending danger. This time though, she wasn't opening it to withdraw from it. She was placing the tapestries in it to ask the chest to reveal what the holes meant in the tapestries.

The chest could only be opened by a combination of incantations and a physical key. The incantations would release the key, which was a part of the intricate carvings on the chest. Moving with deliberation, Odara began the incantations.

"Me, Us, We, call on you, ultimate Mother/Father God, for your infinite wisdom. If you deem it to be necessary and cause-worthy, please release the answers that will provide much needed light for the darkness that encompasses these tapestries. Wehallate, Shistobeh, Tasnidota, Nehabani, Uncalitodia, Yahseh Moteris."

The chest made no sound and didn't move. Odara thought that maybe there wouldn't be a response. Taken aback, thinking she had misread her emotions when touching the fabrics, she was about to stand up and leave the room when the key to the chest began to raise from the carvings on the side of the chest. She waited until it was completely suspended in the air and then took it and opened the chest. She placed the folded tapestries in the chest on top of the other contents and closed it, keeping the key in her hand.

The chest locked on its own, and she heard the contents of it moving around. It turned counterclockwise, and the rumbling of its contents began again. It turned again in the same direction and the rumbling got louder. The chest made one final turn, doing a 180-degree turn to face her, and then there was the sound of several locks clicking open. She used the key to open the final lock and looked inside. Sitting atop of the tapestries were two things: a dreamcatcher—

quite an exquisite one obviously from an American Indian tribe, and there was a scroll. She opened the scroll and it was a map of Africa with Senegal circled. There was a small piece of a tree bark inside of it, no bigger than her hand. Knowing that whatever the chest revealed was never wrong, she was thankful for the help. Still feeling helpless and clueless, she took the dreamcatcher and the scroll out, setting them aside. What happened next was surprising.

Odara reached into the chest to get the tapestries, and when she touched them, she heard a woman's voice crystal clear and firm: "Please help us." She withdrew her hands and felt the heat beginning to fill her palms. She reached for the tapestry on top and asked, "Can you reveal yourself or your location?" This time, the same voice was clear and firm but sounded afraid as it responded, "Many names and many places, please help." The answer set her palms ablaze.

She removed the first tapestry and set it down before reaching for the second one. While pulling it out of the chest, it fell open, and she saw that where there was just two small holes before in the tapestry, there were now several holes in different sections of it. She opened the second one and saw the same thing, only some of the holes were bigger than others and almost looked like they had been torn into the fabric.

Now, she was puzzled. She closed the chest, took what she had retrieved from it into her bedroom, and put it in her closet. She then headed downstairs to have her meal.

When Odara reached the patio to have her early evening meal, the smell of delicious foods greeted her. She sat down at the table facing the courtyard and the acreage, which was a part of the property that she was currently calling home. The view was incredible. The sun was setting, and the land was perfectly manicured and full of beautiful trees, plants, and flowers. She noticed that there were several fruit trees and a vegetable garden in one section. The sight of it all was quite pleasing. While taking in the view, Nicolette, one of the house servants came to the table with a deep red wine, champagne, and freshly brewed coffee. Odara had been so busy looking out at her land that she hadn't noticed the table that was beautifully set. Everything was white and gold, quite like the décor in her bedroom. There was a vase of fresh flowers, orchids, roses, and chrysanthemums in the center of the table. On either side of the vase were candles, which Nicolette lit after pouring the wine and opening the champagne. The linens were crisp and sparkling with gold embroidered edges. When Nicolette returned a few moments later, she brought a mixed green salad, freshly baked bread, butter, and a bowl of soup. "The vegetables are of the finest quality this year, Mademoiselle. Your garden survived the unexpected turns in the weather." Odara blessed her food and placed her napkin on her lap. She tasted the soup first. It was incredible. A simple chicken broth that held the flavors of fresh garlic, basil, and lemongrass. She was delighted. Food was her personal treasure, and well-prepared food was sheer joy. The salad was simple but fresh and equally pleasing with the perfect amount of flavor, courtesy of a homemade pear vinaigrette. As she finished her soup and salad and the first glass of wine, Nicolette reappeared and cleared her plates, pouring another glass of wine for her. She sat and enjoyed the wine, thinking about what the chest had revealed to her and how she couldn't seem to make sense of what she was presented with.

What did an American Indian dreamcatcher have to do with a map of Senegal, and what did the piece of tree branch represent? She would have to go into her garden in the morning and wait for answers through prayer and meditation. In the meantime, she was going to just relax and enjoy the rest of the evening. Whatever was going on was big, and she wanted her night to be easy and carefree, before it began to unfold completely. She was almost startled when Nicolette came back to the table with her dinner. She looked out into the courtyard and saw that there were several lamp posts with candles lit in them. She hadn't even noticed anyone lighting them. Nonetheless, the candlelight amongst the brightly colored flowers in the courtyard was magnificent. She smiled and thanked Nicolette for bringing her meal. She removed the cover from her plate and her mouth watered. Braised lamb chops, roasted potatoes, grilled asparagus, and caramelized carrots. The presentation and the smell alone were enough to intoxicate anyone. She began to eat, and everything on her plate was perfectly seasoned and cooked.

Thanking the Sacred Council again for honoring her request for luxury, she finished her meal and poured herself some champagne. Nicolette came back, cleared all the plates, and then returned with a Crème Brulee for dessert. She poured Odara some of the freshly brewed piping hot coffee and then handed her a light shawl. "For the evening breeze, Mademoiselle." Odara draped the shawl on her shoulders and said thank you. As she was sitting, enjoying her coffee and champagne, she heard the wind speak. Always obedient to all the elements that communicate with her, she looked out into the acreages of land that was within her view. The coffee in her cup began to bubble from the heat in her hand, which quickly escalated to fiery hot.

Odara sat staring, unable to move. Without blinking, she looked across all her land. There were Black women everywhere. They were standing, facing her with blank facial expressions. Thousands of them. Standing side by side, all ages, all sizes, and all skin tones wearing clothing from a multitude of time periods. They were silent, and they were just standing there staring at her. She stood up and took a couple of steps towards the patio gate.

They didn't move a muscle, and they weren't responding to any of the questions she was asking telepathically. She followed them row by row with her eyes and noticed that in the middle of them was a large group, all similarly dressed. That group also had more women who appeared to be closer in age to one another. While looking at that group, she felt the fire of rage, the depth of battle, and a sense of despair. Before she could ask them how she could she help or what they needed from her, they were gone. In the blink of an eye, her grounds were the same flower and tree filled grounds she was admiring earlier. She sank to the ground and asked the earth for a sign. The stillness that followed her request was stifling. Giselle and Nicolette appeared by her side and helped her to her feet. Without a word spoken, they walked with her upstairs to her bedroom, each one with a reassuring arm around her waist. After she got in the bed, Giselle spoke, "Your task is mighty this time, Mademoiselle. I will prepare your herbal tea first thing in the morning before you grace your garden for answers." Odara looked at her and realized that Giselle bore an uncanny resemblance to Mutora, her first earthly mother. When she looked up again to thank her, Giselle was gone. Drained, Odara fell quickly into a deep sleep.

Odara looked around the marketplace to determine where she would start. The smell of fresh ground coffee beans drew her to the street vendor who had a large variety of ground and unground beans. He immediately began to boast of his beans being the freshest, the most flavorful, and the highest quality. He quickly prepared an espresso for her to sample. He was right. As soon as she tasted it, she knew that she had to make her first purchase with him. After buying a small variety of beans in quarter pound portions, she turned to survey the area again. A small setup with beautifully colored silk scarves caught her eye. She began to make her way across the cobblestone street to see them up close, and she heard the unmistakable sound of women weeping. Looking in all directions and seeing no one, she kept walking across the street. As she approached the vendor's stall, she glanced to her right. Her palms instantly went ablaze as she saw two elderly women, possibly twins, on their knees. Rocking back and forth, weeping, and they had their hands outstretched to her. She took a couple of steps towards them and they vanished.

"Wait!" she yelled out, before she was jolted out of her sleep by the sound of her own voice. She sat straight up in her bed. The dream was yet another cry for help. She looked at her palms and they were almost glowing from the temperature of them. None of the pieces fit. *What in the world is going on*? She laid back on her pillows and slowly drifted back to sleep.

When the winds change direction

3
The Shift/ Reassigned

When the morning sun began to fill Odara's bedroom, she turned over to see the beauty of it filtering into the room. No sooner than her eyes had opened, Giselle entered the room with a tray set for tea. Thanking her, and still in a somewhat shaken state from the dream she had, or rather, the message that she'd received, Odara chose to lay still for a few more minutes. When she got up to go to the bathroom and shower, she thought she heard a doorbell. Not quite sure who on earth it could be, she dismissed it as probably a delivery.

She showered and dressed quickly, opting for a long white flowing skirt and a pretty white silk halter top. She went to her garden to do some meditating and praying while waiting to receive her next assignment. She put on her slippers and was walking to the French doors that led to the balcony stairs when Giselle re-entered the room. "Mademoiselle Odara, you have a visitor in the drawing room." Odara was not going to be distracted from getting her instructions from the garden, so she told Giselle to let them know she was busy and to come back later in the day.

"With all due respect, Mademoiselle, I cannot do that. The visitor in the drawing room is Phillip." Odara froze where she stood. *Phillip! The messenger for the Sacred Council?! What in the world is going on around here?* Despite her shock, she was thrilled. Phillip was one of her favorite people to interact with. He only came when there was something of extreme importance to be delivered or shared, and of course, when someone was being promoted. The last time she saw him, she was being promoted. He handed her the promotion personally and waited for the full transformation to who she was now. A warrior for the second sentry. There was only one level higher than that and she was certain she hadn't done anything to earn another promotion since she had last seen him. She powdered her face and put on some lipstick and pearl earrings before hurriedly heading downstairs to greet him.

As soon as she entered the room, Giselle was right behind her with the tray that was set up for tea, now a service for two. Leaving and closing the drawing room door, Giselle smiled and retreated. Phillip was once again a sight to behold. One of the finest Black men you would ever lay eyes on and always immaculately and impeccably dressed. Always formal, he donned a black velvet jacket with a jacquard vest, sparkling white shirt with an ascot that matched his vest, black silk trousers, and black shoes with white spats. He was wearing a hat and had a white rose in his lapel. When he reached out to hug her, the diamonds in his cufflinks sparkled in the light.

Odara gave him a warm hug and then sat down to receive whatever news he had for her. She poured them both some tea but instead of sitting down, he walked over to the fireplace and asked, "May I?" Odara responded with, "Of course," and he lit the logs that were in the fireplace already prepared for burning. Now she was becoming even more curious. Phillip wasn't one for creature comforts. His sole human affinity was the finest clothing from whatever time period he was sent to do work. After the fire was lit, with his back still turned to her, he began to speak. "There has been a major shift in several different realms and time periods simultaneously. You are being temporarily reassigned. The Sacred Council has deemed you, and only you, as capable of handling this assignment because you still *"feel"* things. What needs to be handled requires someone who is well skilled in spiritual warfare, physical battle, and handling emotional distress and loss. Someone who can execute themselves fully as a spiritual warrior and as a human being without confusing the two. Your new assignment will require you to execute in both spirit and flesh, sometimes at the same time." He turned to face her and opened a small box. He took out three small sparkling stones and put them in the fire. "I am sure that you have questions because you wouldn't be you if you did not. I do not have answers, only your orders to travel immediately." Phillip walked back over to the fireplace and stuck his hand in the fire, retrieving the stones that were now fiery red. He came and sat next to Odara and placed them in her teacup. He then poured them both teas. "Drink up, you will need the fire that you were created from during this next journey more than once, and you will need to be in more than one place at a time. The stones were blessed by Isis, touched by Shango, and Kali laced them with control of time. You have been chosen once again for something that affects not only this planet and realm, but the alignment of all universal life sources. When I leave, so will you, and you will know exactly what to do, as well as how you are to do it. What kind of tea is this? It smells delicious."

Odara sipped her tea as she had been told and felt the fire from the stones coursing through her body. It was an incredible feeling, the power of fire. She allowed herself to feel it from the top of her head to the bottom of her feet. She was being strengthened. From what Phillip had just shared, she was going to need it. "The tea is called Oolong. It is from China." Phillip sat, and they shared their tea in silence. He stood up and said, "When you finish your new assignment, you will return to this place and finish the work that needs to be done here." He then walked to the door, tipped his hat, and was gone.

Odara sat, staring at the spot where Phillip had just stood, processing everything that he had shared with her. She felt a quickening in her body as the energy from the stones in the tea continued to spread through her. She thought about the dream, the voice asking for help, the women on her land, and what the chest revealed to her. A sense of dread, sadness, and helplessness washed over her. It wasn't her feelings she felt, it was the feelings of the women she had seen. Giselle entered the room and stood by the door, holding a small box.

Odara motioned for her to come all the way in and she handed Odara the box. "For your companion, Mademoiselle." *Another twist!? What companion? I always work alone!* She didn't verbalize the questions in her head. She just accepted the box and said thank you. She opened the box and inside of it was a small jeweled collar, obviously for a small pet. She didn't even have the time to try to figure it out.

She had to prepare her body for time travel and pack a small bag with some of what she would need when she got to where she was going. She headed up the stairs to go to her personal garden outside of her bedroom, and when she looked back, Giselle and Nicolette were at the foot of the stairs. Mutora and Roma, "Thank you," she said aloud. They nodded and smiled at her. "I am preparing myself for flight and battle. My first stop is the Augustin House." Giselle and Nicolette now clearly recognizable as Mutora and Roma instantly dropped to their knees. Odara was taken aback. "Is there something I should know that hasn't been revealed yet?" Giselle spoke without looking up, "The Augustin House is a Holy Place. Whatever you are being called to do is of great importance. Listen to yourself, and if you need to summon the Sacred Council, do so.

You are fully prepared and capable of handling whatever it is, but do not doubt yourself at any time. Anything that has come against that house that warrants a warrior from the second sentry to step in and fight is something of great evil. Show yourself, Odara!

You will need all of your capabilities for this one." Odara looked at them both on their knees with their heads bowed. She felt full love and respect for the two women who were a part of her creation a thousand years ago. She took a step then turned back to them and said, "I will keep a portal open in case I need your assistance, and I will unseal my pantry for you to retrieve whatever is necessary in the event that I call on you." They both looked up at her and nodded as she headed to her bedroom.

When Odara entered her bedroom, she immediately began taking off all her clothes. When she finished undressing, she took a moment to admire the painting of the angel that looked like a portrait of her beloved Jerod. The painting was not there. She stood there blinking at the spot where the painting was, and in its place was a full sized very ornate mirror. The smile that came to her lips as she stood looking into the mirror became full. At the exact same moment, she heard the ruffling of feathers and saw Jerod standing behind her in the reflection of the mirror. She turned around to embrace him, but he wasn't there. There was a bundle of feathers neatly tied with a purple ribbon and a red rose sitting on her bed. She knew that he was gifting her aid in her time travels and for defense. A feather from an angel wing could immobilize any human being when being used by a warrior from the spirit realm. "Thank you, Beloved," she said aloud. She went to her closet and pulled out a white caftan. She was about to go outside to her garden to bathe in the magic of its contents when she was redirected. "The pantry is where you will be prepared this time." She recognized the unmistakable voice of Shango, the God of Thunder, and the room shook from its power. She took the scroll and the dreamcatcher out of the closet where she had placed them and went from her bedroom to the door of the dressing room.

Quickly, Odara placed her palm on the door and used the incantation that opens the Spirit lock. Once inside of the dressing room, she set down the scroll and the dreamcatcher and stretched both of her arms out. She needed to locate her secret pantry, and she hadn't had the time to allow it to call out for her presence. With her arms outstretched, she closed her eyes and said, "Reveal yourself. I am in need of physical preparation for travel and warfare in both physical and spirit form!" She heard what sounded like a large piece of furniture being moved across a floor and the sound of wind chimes. Then there was silence. Odara opened her eyes, and the door to the secret pantry was in the middle of the wall where the closet once stood.

The secret pantry would be considered any herbalist or natural healers' heaven. Temperature controlled and spacious. It had shelves and drawers full of powders, roots, bulbs, and elixirs. To the natural eye, it would just look like someone was heavy into natural healing remedies. It was so much more than that. In this pantry, she would sometimes spend hours preparing things at the small table in the center of it. Along with what she had harvested in her own garden, there were roots and herbs only heard of through folklore in this pantry. There were also considerable amounts of things that grew from the earth that no one in this planetary realm would recognize. To top it all off, there was a numerable amount of exquisite plant leaves and dried fruits from other dimensions that could be very dangerous and even deadly if any curious human or devious spirit got ahold of them.

Everything in this pantry had been handpicked by the eldest and most superior of healers that served the Sacred Council. Odara always knew when they were in her pantry adding something amazing before they greeted her with instructions and blessings. The aroma that followed them wherever they went was one that couldn't be contained by any earthly room nor could it be mistaken. It was a heavenly smell that reeked with the smell of fresh earth mixed with musk and floral notes. Whenever she smelled that scent, she was elated. She knew that she was being gifted, and that gift came with more power, education, and another skill set. Sometimes it was just a small root, sometimes it was a bundle of bulbs, and sometimes it was an entire shelf of things. Every time, it was fascinating. What she needed from the pantry today were things that could be of use in physical battle, things that would be useful in case she ran into someone who had been inhabited by demonic or evil forces.

Odara walked into the pantry and closed the door behind her. The pantry had doubled in size from the last time she had been inside of it. She was certain that it was because her recent promotion granted her access to more options for anything she would need. She walked around the room and looked at all the shelves. Everything was so orderly and appeared to just be a room full of plants and roots in jars and pots. She took a white linen cloth down from a shelf and covered the small table in the center of the room. Then she picked up a velvet satchel and untied the silk cord that held it together. Once opened, she spread the satchel out on top of the linen.

"Asking for assistance and immediate understanding of what I am to receive, my travel will take place when I leave this room. Humbly, I beseech of your selections to aid in ensuring my success in the completion of this assignment. I have been told that I will have battle and warfare in spirit and in flesh along with being present in more than one realm at one time. This time, I am asking not for something for someone else. What I need from you is for me, Born Machaneka now in the body of Odara, spiritual warrior for the second sentry of the Sacred Council."

Odara sat down on the floor in lotus position and prepared to wait for a response. Normally, anywhere from five minutes to an hour was how long it could possibly take. That day, the response was instantaneous. The contents on the shelving in the pantry began to rearrange itself, some sliding forward from behind other jars. Some of the empty jars began to fill with a combination of bulbs, roots, and herbs, and they began to chop and blend before turning into powders. Shelves and cubbies began to exchange places. She had never seen the pantry respond so quickly *and so aggressively.* During the process, the sound of a singing bowl filled the room. It continued until the room stopped rearranging itself. When everything was completely still, Odara stood up and walked over to the shelving. Everything that she would need had been pushed forward to stand alone in its perspective place. The purpose for the contents of each jar would reveal itself as soon as she touched it. She was surprised to see that out of all of that banging, clanging, and rearranging, there were only two jars pushed forward on one shelf. She reached for the first jar and took it down. It contained Brugmansia, also known as Angels Trumpets; it was powdered and to be used in food or tea. When ingested, it would cause someone to lose connection with reality and cause hallucinations. Too much was fatal. She opened the jar and took the small pouch out and placed it on the table in the center of the outspread satchel. She went back over to the shelf and reached for the second jar. It contained a salve in a small tin from Amaterasu, the Japanese Sun Goddess. She was to use it on her hands to contain the fire that she would become during the assignment. Placing the salve in the satchel as well, Odara tied the satchel with the purple cord and then around her waist. She thanked the pantry for its assistance and then remembered that she needed to leave it unlocked for Giselle and Nicolette, in case she needed further assistance from them. In her human form, she needed incantations and a ritual to get permission for someone else to have access, but in spirit form, all she needed to do was command the room. She didn't have time to go through the ritual, so she sat down in the chair at the table and closed her eyes.

"Ascend now!" she said aloud. There was a swirl of wind and light that encircled her as her spirit left the body of Odara. Once completely free of her body, the singing bowl began to fill the room with sound. "Mutora and Roma have my permission to enter in my absence to gather what they need to assist me for this assignment. There is nothing they cannot access. Assemble for them and provide whatever they seek, should they enter." Everything in the pantry began to illuminate. Access had been granted. Her spirit re-entered her body and Odara stood up and left the room.

When she came out of the pantry, Odara quickly changed into the purple gown that she was given by the Sacred Council for her promotion. She put the amethyst amulet that Mutora had given her around her neck. She grabbed the map, the dreamcatcher, and the feathers Jerod had left her. She then walked to her bedroom to the balcony overlooking her most prized possession, her garden. She walked down the stairs to the center of the garden and sat down, where a small altar and pillow were permanently stationed. Looking around at the different sections, she was flooded with memories of what assignments had called for each herb, sometimes combinations of them. Rosemary, Lavender, Feverfew, Basil, Apple Blossom, Chamomile, Sandalwood, Goldenseal, Eucalyptus, Belladonna, Clover, Frankincense, Comfrey, Buckeye, Patchouli, Purslane, Sage, Thyme, Tobacco, Valerian, Mug Wort, Mandrake, and Hyssop. They were sectioned by purpose: protection and purification; cleansing and detox; prophecy and divination; love and attraction; sedation and defense. Her understanding of each one and the full potential of their power was extensive. The deities that represented them were always given full respect while tending to them. Her garden was a sacred place and could only be entered by permission. The first step into her garden must be hers if she was with someone. The entire garden had been blessed and set up for the sole purpose of aiding her in her assignments.

Because of this, if a stranger set foot into it without Odara leading, everything in it would retreat into the earth until she bid it to grow again. The plants, flowers, and herbs were designed for spiritual warfare and could not be touched by humans without being released by her. They were not your grocery or nursery variety, planted for viewing pleasure. They were, however, a pleasure to behold. Simply because they were infused with spirit and life.

The earth that they sprang from was tilled and prepared with the dirt and water from sacred lands, untouched by any natural human hand. Standing in the center of the garden looking like a Goddess, Odara in her new stronger form was a sight to behold. As she looked around, the sage plants began to emit clouds of aroma and the lavender followed suit. She was being acknowledged and purified at the same time. She called out the wind for the first leg of her journey. "Swiftly to the Augustin house, St Maarten, two hundred- and twenty-five-years South." The wind obliged her immediately. She was swept up, and in flight through centuries of time, headed to the Augustin House. Home of the family of women who were entrusted to weave the tapestries of life for all time, by the ultimate creator who some people referred to as God.

Anything but ordinary

4
Sunday Dinner

Odara landed at the end of the road that lead to the Augustin House. The view from where she stood was majestic. The landscape with the house in the middle of it was beautiful. A small peach orchard, Magnolia trees, white roses, and manicured hedges were perfectly placed. The road was paved and lined with Bougainvillea of all colors. She inhaled the fresh island air and realized that her clothing hadn't assumed the culture of the time period. So be it. She was ready to engage and find out what was going on behind the doors of the house. She began walking down the paved road to the house.

There wasn't a neighboring house in sight and no one on the two roads that led to the house. She had expected to feel some sort of trouble or dissention once she arrived, but what she felt more and more of as she approached the front door was a strong sense of deep love. Interesting, considering all the disturbing messages she had received prior to getting there.

As she got closer to the house, the smell of what had to be a fantastic meal being prepared began to get stronger and stronger. She was hungry. Time travel always left her famished. Before she knew it, she was at the front door. She knocked loudly on the solid wood door and stepped back. A young woman dressed in servant's clothing opened the door. "Welcome, Ms. Odara, please come in." Odara was startled. Never in a thousand years had anyone known who she was before she told them and never had anyone been expecting her. This was most definitely a whole new level of assignment. "Thank you," she replied to the young woman. She stepped into the house and followed the woman from the foyer into a large sitting room. "Please sit. Ma'am Bessie and Ma'am Ethel B will be glad to know that you have arrived. I'm certain you must be hungry.

You picked the perfect day to arrive. Sunday dinner in the Augustin home is a welcome worth reckoning with. My name is Rose Alecia, and I am your personal attendant during your stay here. There is nothing I cannot get or do for you. Nothing. You may call me Lisa if you should like to. When Samara was a small girl, she couldn't say my full name, so she started calling me that, and it kind of caught on."

Odara, now seeing through her spiritual eyes, looked at Rose Alecia and saw the protective veil and sparkling aura that encompassed the body of her attendant. She is not of this place. She wasn't an Angel but clearly not fully human either. Her presence was warm and kind but beneath that was an undercurrent of power and strength. Fair skinned, wavy hair pulled neatly into a bun in the back of her head, and small in stature, Rose Alecia looked harmless and submissive. Odara knew by what she was feeling from looking at her that there was an entirely different spirit in that body. *What in the world is going on here?* Odara smiled at her and said thank you as Lisa poured her a cup of water and then seemingly disappeared. Literally.

Odara had just finished drinking her water and was setting the cup down on the cocktail table when she looked up and saw the twin matriarchs standing in the doorway. Her cup missed the table and fell to the floor. The two elderly women from the dream! The ones who were on their knees weeping and reaching out for help in the marketplace! Lisa appeared and picked the cup up from the floor. She smiled and said, "Ms. Addie says dinner will be served in thirty minutes." Then she was gone again.

The taller one, Bessie, spoke first. "We knew you would come! We sent you messages and we knew you would come. The other twin, Ethel B, spoke softly, "We saw you while we were praying, and we knew that you would be the one to help. And now you're here. We are grateful for what you are going to do to help. It's quite a bit, you know. It's so much that we couldn't even see it all. For the first time in forty years, we broke the cycle of constant prayer to greet you. Let us embrace you and transfer what we know before dinner. It will help you to understand the conversations that my nieces will probably be having as we dine.

After dinner, I must return to prayer position when Bessie goes back to work." Odara stood and walked over to them. They were paternal twins. One tall and the other not so much, one milk chocolate brown and the other the color of a golden sunset. Both had silver hair neatly combed, and they both had eyes that seemed to see through to your soul. They reached out to hug her and the candles in the room began to flicker. Odara put her arms around them both and received a very chilling download. Their energy was strong, fluid, and tangible. They allowed her to access their hearts and minds as they stood wrapped up together. When they released her from the embrace, she felt like she couldn't believe what she had just learned. She stood there holding their hands with tears running down her face. Bessie spoke again, "You can do this; we know you can."

Bessie and Ethel stared at Odara with hopeful, reassuring eyes. Turning at the same time in the uncanny way that twins sometimes do things, they began to walk out of the room. Bessie beckoned her to follow them. They walked down the hallway to a formal dining room. As she was seated, Ethel told Lisa to let the girls know that it was time to join them for dinner and that they had a guest. Odara was still digesting what she had learned from the matriarchs. She was also still processing that *everyone* in this house was special, gifted, or not of this realm. This was a lot. She knew what she would need to do to get started, but she wasn't going to do anything until she summoned the Sacred Council. Probably later that night after dinner.

A wave of power coming from the hallway began to filter into the dining room. Through her human eyes, what Odara was seeing was amazing. Through the eyes of the spirit warrior that she was, Odara saw the fullness of power and grace enter the room before the physical entrance of "the girls" as their Aunt Ethel B referred to them. The shine from the stars in the night sky that were visible from the dining room window almost doubled. The candles on the two candelabras that were lit began to glow with ferocity. The potted plants and flowers throughout the room stood up and seemed to fan out in welcome. Along with all of that, everything in the room appeared to be brighter, livelier, and almost magical.

They entered the room in the same order that they were born. Intisar, Glenda, the twins Linda and Ola, then Zora, and lastly, the ball of fire that was the youngest, Samara. *"Girls!"* she thought and almost said aloud. This was an entire team of powerful women. Intisar took a seat at the head of the table. She was almost six feet tall, lean, and strong looking. Dressed in a long yellow skirt and a white blouse with a yellow flower in her reddish-brown afro, she had a smile in her eyes but a very serious look on her face. Glenda was a dark brown-skinned woman, somewhat shorter than Intisar but carrying the same magnetism and formality in mannerisms. She was wearing a print skirt and a flowing orange blouse that made the chocolate in her skin glow. Zora came in behind Glenda wearing a long bright green dress, large gold earrings, and lots of gold bangles and rings on both of her arms and hands. Linda and Ola, true to twin form, entered walking in unison wearing deep purple long velvet skirts, royal blue silk blouses, and layered pearl necklaces. Samara, the youngest of the sisters came in walking as if she was on air. She moved so smoothly that she looked like she was floating. She was the fairest skinned of them all and had a lion's mane of an afro that had been combed through and adorned with gold beads and cowrie shells in the center of her forehead adorning her crown. She wore a white evening gown and was the only one wearing makeup. Her eyes had been outlined with a dark liner, and on her lips, she wore a color that looked like blackberries. When they were all seated at the table, Odara inhaled and sat in awe of the range of style, the depth of their beauty, and the overwhelming energy that radiated from them. Things were getting more interesting with every moment. She hadn't ever felt this kind of regal power and energy in one room at the same time. These were the women who were responsible for capturing the life stories of every person in the universe in their tapestries and no two were alike. Even the twins. Linda was a very calm, quiet spirit while Ola was an explosion waiting to happen. She loved them immediately. All of them. The only thing she could think was that she had to help them. She was determined that before she left that incredible house, she would do whatever it took to get the assignment completed and restore the order that was needed.

Before Ms. Bessie could formally introduce them, Samara sent her a message. "I'm so glad that you are here. It's quite frustrating and draining what's been happening, and Mama nor Aunt Ethel B will tell us what they know. I know who you are. I see you in the stars sometimes. I am honored that we're blessed with your assistance." Odara looked her directly in the eyes and responded between them. "You're telepathic?" Samara responded,"Of course I am. We all are. My sisters just won't access it and they get upset when I read their minds. I really can't help it. I can't read Mama's though, or Aunt Ethel B's. God said they were off limits." Odara smiled at the twenty something year old with the same eyes as the mighty Isis of the Sacred Council. "So, you talk to God is what you're telling me?" Samara didn't blink or take her eyes off Odara. "You have to if you do the work that we do. I talk to him all of the time. She delivers my threads to me personally, you know." Odara stared at her, taking it all in. "She?" Samara giggled and said, "Yessssss, SHE. I see a woman, Intisar sees a man, the twins get light and wind, Glenda sees an older man, and Zora doesn't see, she just feels the presence. You get what you can understand best. Ever changing. That's what Mama says." Before Odara could respond, Lisa entered with a serving cart, and the smell of Sunday dinner took over the room.

Intisar watched Samara and Odara closely, then she spoke firmly and quietly. "What you're doing is rude, Samara. Conversations at our dinner table should be held aloud." To which Samara quickly chirped back, "I was just sharing a little information. I'll stop now." Intisar smiled at her and said, "I know you can't help it. We bore you with our lack of participation in communicating that way. Thank you for ceasing." Lisa and Addie who were the cooks, began to place steaming hot platters of food on the table. Oxtails, jerk chicken, rice and peas, plantain, sweet bread, cabbage, and bread pudding. Enough for a small village. As Lisa was pouring lemonade and water for everyone, Ms. Bessie commanded the room by telling everyone to bow their heads for grace. After the food was blessed and all the plates were full, conversation began to flow. Listening intently, Odara noted that they were very respectful of each other while communicating. No one butted in or asked questions about anything someone was saying until that person paused from speaking or stopped completely. They gave each other their undivided attention as each one shared whatever was on their mind. Ms. Ethel B addressed Odara, "This meal is the only full meal that we share all week. Every day at 5 a.m., we get up with the sun and have tea together. We're sustained by that tea throughout the week until time for dinner on Sunday. I know it sounds odd, but it works quite effectively. We get so full of the work that we do, no one develops an appetite. We feed off the energy of our tapestries." Odara was intoxicated by the combination of the magnitude of where she was, who these women were, what she was feeling and the food in front of her. She decided to keep quiet, let it all sink in, and enjoy dinner.

After they all finished eating, Samara told Odara that the evening breeze and the smell of the fresh flowers surrounding the house was something to behold. The sisters excused themselves and left the room in the same order that they came in, eldest to youngest. Aunt Ethel B took her hand and said, "Depending on how long you're here, you won't see my sister and I at the same time except for Sunday dinners. We had the guest room prepared for you with special care for your comfort. When you're ready to lie down, Rose Alecia will show you to it." And then she was gone. Sitting quietly, she heard a main door and then several other doors close. Odara decided to go outside and sit in the front yard, on the bench under the Magnolia tree, to enjoy the night breeze that Samara mentioned. She needed to summon the Sacred Council through communion with the moon and it seemed like the perfect spot.

As she approached the tree, Odara saw that a light blanket and a lantern were already in place.

Beside the bench was a small table that had a steaming pot and a teacup next to it. She sat down and let the evening breeze and the smell of the flowers from the tree and the front yard take over her. She took out the dreamcatcher and the map of Senegal and looked them over and over. Instead of immediately going into incantation to summon the Sacred Council, she stood up and hung the dreamcatcher on a low hanging branch of the tree. It was quite an impressive piece, and she smiled as it began to blow gently in the wind. She sat back down on the bench, poured a cup of tea, and watched it swing freely in the evening breeze. She went over in her mind exactly what she was going to say to the Sacred Council. She heard the ruffling of feathers and sat straight up in expectation of Jerod possibly appearing, but he didn't. Instead, the wind increased dramatically, a strong gust blew the dreamcatcher off the limb, into the air, and down a road that lead from the main road to the house. Seeing the direction that it flew, Odara transferred herself with warp speed to the end of the road to catch it. Her body reached the end of the road with her arms extended to catch the dreamcatcher in motion, but it wasn't there. She looked around slightly puzzled and felt a presence that was unfamiliar and strangely familiar at the same time. Looking down, she almost laughed aloud. A beautiful black Persian cat was sitting next to her feet with the dreamcatcher in its mouth. He was looking at her with a smile in his eyes and staring intently like he wanted to be picked up. She swooped him up into her arms and took the dreamcatcher from him.

"Thank you, Sir, and what might be your name?" Odara asked. The cat snuggled up against her and responded directly to her mind, "My name is Prentice, and I have been sent to assist you. It's been a long day. You're prettier than I anticipated. I have several sets of powers and gifts that you will need and I'm cold and hungry. You will never have to call for me or instruct me. I will automatically assume the proper position for any situation. And don't be alarmed when Samara knows who and what I am, she's very special, you know." Odara looked into his eyes and saw the heavens with swirling clouds reflected in them. She stroked his fur for a few moments and remembered the collar Giselle had given to her. She removed it from the satchel tied around her waist and set Prentice down. "I believe this is for you, Prentice." He sat patiently still as she put the collar around his neck and adjusted it. It was quite the exquisite piece. The jewels that graced it sparkled intensely. When she stepped back to admire it, Prentice looked up at her and said, "Watch."

In the next few moments, she was definite that Prentice was a gift from the Sacred Council. Prentice stood up and walked in a circle, twice, then sat back down. He looked up at Odara and tilted his head sideways. Within a few seconds, he was standing next to her in her form, identical from head to toe. While she gasped in disbelief, he crouched down and assumed the form of a Phoenix, then a tree, then a fireball, then a doorway, then a small dragon. Odara was rendered speechless as he did a final transition back to a black Persian cat.

He smiled at her and said aloud, "Anything I assume in form, I also assume the capacity to do whatever it is capable of with that capacity multiplied by 1000, and anything that I assume in form enables you to multiply yourself as necessary." Odara got down on one knee and stroked him again. "Let's get to the house, Prentice. We have work to do."

Together, they walked back to the Magnolia tree where Odara was sitting when the wind kicked up. She picked up the blanket, put out the lantern light, and headed back to the house. Prentice walked beside her, keeping pace with her stride. He was a very handsome, striking black cat. Even his walk was regal. She was pleased and thankful for his presence and intrigued by the gifts and powers that he possessed.

Before she could open the front door, Lisa opened it and welcomed her back inside. “I will show you to your room. There is also a bed prepared for your companion.” Odara followed silently. No need to ponder how Lisa knew that she would be returning with a guest. Nothing about this home was normal or predictable.

They were led to a bedroom that was as comfortable as it was beautiful, everything soft and richly colored. A nightgown and robe were lain across the foot of the bed and a beautiful scarlet-colored large pillow was graced with a gold blanket on the floor for Prentice. She looked at him and he climbed into his resting spot and began to get situated while she undressed and got into the bed. Within minutes they were both sleeping peacefully.

5
The Weavers at Work

The morning sun began to filter through the curtains and Odara began to awaken when she felt the warmth of it on her face. She decided to lie still while recapturing the events of the day before in her mind. So much in one day and she still didn't fully know what her assignment entailed. "We're prepared and no doubt will be successful," the voice in her head, speaking with formal conviction startled her. It was Prentice, communicating telepathically. She had almost forgotten that he was there. She sat up in the bed and saw him curled up in his bed, on the floor licking his paws. Odara responded aloud, "This is bigger than anything I've ever encountered. I'm sure of it, because my call is the burning in my hands; it hasn't ceased for one second since I was redirected to this assignment." Prentice stopped licking his paws and looked at her. "Are you afraid?" he asked. "No, just leery of what awaits," she responded. As she began to get out of the bed, she noticed there were a few dresses hung on the closet door that resembled quite closely what she was wearing when she arrived. Beginning to see that no details had been spared for her comfort, Odara chose an orange dress that had gold embroidered threads around the neck, waistline, and ends of the sleeves. After bathing and dressing, she picked Prentice up and headed down the hall. Today was the day to visit each of the sisters in their own element. She needed to find out what was going on there that was so important, that she was pulled from one assignment and placed there.

When Odara entered the great room holding Prentice, Lisa greeted her with a pot of coffee, a tray of biscuits, and a bowl of milk. Odara told Lisa she would wait for the others and didn't want to be rude. "They have tea every morning at 5 a.m. sharp, Ms. Odara. After that, you will not see them unless you are in their work chambers. The next time everyone dines will be for Sunday dinner. When you have had your coffee, I will show you to the workshop." She turned to Prentice and said, "I sweetened the milk for you. I hope it is to your liking." Prentice jumped out of Odara's arms and began to lap at the milk in his bowl. After a moment, he sat up on his hind legs and stared at Lisa. "You're quite welcome," she said and exited the room.

Odara sipped on her coffee and watched Prentice slowly devour his bowl of milk. He was fascinating to watch. She believed that he was quite the charming character. "Do you always communicate with the humans in your midst, telepathically or otherwise? she asked. Prentice continued to drink his milk and didn't look her way. Odara snickered to herself, *now he's going to ignore me*. Prentice finished his milk and turned to face her. "I do not even try unless I'm sure they are from the spirit world. However, in this house, nothing is normal. We're in a house full of gifted folks from other realms who've been designed to be a family. I think it's extraordinary." Odara allowed herself to take in what Prentice had said and then called for Lisa. "I'm ready to visit these incredible women now."

Lisa guided Odara through the house and outside to the cottage that was the workshop. From the outside, it appeared to be a simple flat with lots of heavily curtained windows. When they got to the front door, Lisa opened it for Odara and Prentice. There was a small foyer and then a hallway. Lisa extended her arm pointing down the hall. "You will find everyone in their own spaces. Ms. Bessie or Ms. Ethel B will be in the prayer closet at the back of the house. You will only be able to speak with them one at a time. They are all expecting you. Be mindful that you may sense many emotions while in their spaces. The work they do has become a part of them." Prentice jumped down from Odara's arms and stood looking down the hallway. He looked up at Odara and relaxed into sitting position. "This is for you to experience. I'll wait here." Odara stared down the hallway as well. The energy in this cottage was tangible. She could feel different emotions, almost hear them, coming from behind the door of every room. Taking a deep breath and a second glance at Prentice, she walked to the first door at the beginning of the hallway and opened it.

"Welcome! Please come in and close the door behind you," Intisar greeted her without looking away from her work. Odara came in and took a seat by the window in a large comfortable chair. There was a rocking chair on the other side of it. She started to sit there but she felt as if she wasn't supposed to sit in it. After she had been seated for a couple of minutes, Intisar began to speak, "My mother and Aunt Ethel B sent for you through prayer. I have had some difficulties with my work recently that is seemingly progressing. Thank you for not sitting in the rocking chair. When God shows up here, that is his preferred resting place." Odara was silent.

She now understood why the rocking chair seemed present but unavailable for her to sit in. She watched Intisar intently. Intisar Augustin was a tall, stately, mocha-colored woman with a beautiful full head of reddish blonde afro. She was strikingly beautiful with a genuine deep smile and eyes that seemed to look through you. Her presence was serious but not intimidating, strong but not intrusive, and you could feel her mind spinning with thoughts. Seeing that Odara had no response for her, she continued to speak. "The tapestry that I am responsible for is for those who have or will exist on planet Earth in any dimension or time. As of late, I've been becoming growingly frustrated by my work. Can you come over here and watch for a few minutes so I can show you why?" Odara got up and stood next to Intisar at her loom. She watched in awe and fascination as Intisar's hands maneuvered the threads on the loom with precision and speed. "Do you know whose lives you're weaving into the tapestry? Or rather can you feel what the threads are saying?" Odara asked. "I can feel the emotions that accompany the events of their lives. Sadness, joy, peace, anger – but I don't get faces or identities if that's what you're asking. And here is why I needed you to come watch," Intisar replied. "Look." Intisar stopped all motion and waited for Odara to see what she needed her to see. Odara started at the bottom of the pattern and scanned it with her eyes. As she got halfway into it, she noticed a couple of small holes. She blinked and they seemed to be getting larger! She kept working her way visually through the tapestry and saw a few other holes sporadically in different areas. Some small, some larger, some clustered, and some spread out. She was taken aback. Not because there were holes in the tapestry, but because they were forming and spreading on their own right before her eyes. She felt the beginning of heat in her palms as she studied the tapestry, watching the holes form right before her eyes. The heat began to intensify as she followed the beautiful pattern that was being disrupted by the holes. The image of the small tapestries that she found neatly folded in her closet at the chateau came to her mind; remembering the holes and how they appeared to have multiplied in size right in front of her on her bedroom floor. Her palms were almost ablaze. She felt a sudden rush of sadness and then fear. The fear wasn't hers, it was coming from the cloth on the loom. She looked at Intisar. Intisar was staring out of the window that she worked by, humming. A couple of tears rolled from the corner of her eye. "Even though I don't get the actual identity of the people whose lives I'm recording, I do know if they're male or female, adult or child, and I know what culture they represent. All the holes are appearing in family lines where women are being recorded. They are women who have been displaced, who I believe are missing. Something on this earth in another dimension is attacking African American women—stealing them—and there is nothing being done about it. That is why the holes are growing in numbers. I have counted 64,000 holes in the last year." Intisar sat, continuing to stare out of the window. "Some of these women were heading for greatness and change in the world as a result of their lives, and the lives of those in their lineage. That has been disrupted, and it is throwing off the balance of the natural course of progression for the planet, possibly the universe. Someone must find out why this is happening, and also find out who or what is responsible for it and stop it. If the tapestries begin to fall apart, so will the lives and families of the women who have been abducted. And it will spread to the lives and families of all those connected to them. En masse, there will be confusion, chaos, anger, and eventually destruction. The spirit and energies of Black women play a critical role in the fabric of life. She is under attack and the responsible evil must be stopped. We believe that someone who can do that is you." Odara was lost for words. 64,000 Black women missing in America. What part of America, what time period, how does that happen and grow without action? She felt herself becoming angry and looked at Intisar staring out of the window. As statuesque and powerful as she appeared when Odara first entered the room, she now looked helpless and almost defeated.

Odara put her hand on Intisar's shoulder. "I am being told our visit is over. I do not believe I need to visit your sisters today. I have much to address. Be not fearful, Intisar, this will not continue." Odara walked out of the room and closed the door behind her. Prentice stood to his feet when he saw her. She walked past him and headed down the hall and back into the yard for the main house. She stopped to feel the breeze from the morning air and let the wind speak to her. What she heard was daunting: "There is no time, be swift." Odara picked Prentice up and said, "We have a trip to take, Prentice. The knowledge that we need for this next leg is not here." Prentice purred and jumped from her arms. She was about to scoop him up again when he vanished. "I don't have time to play, Prentice!" Before she could say another word to chastise him, he reappeared. In his mouth was the scroll that had presented itself when she called for help from her sacred chest. He dropped the scroll, and the small piece of tree bark that was wrapped in it fell out. "I believe our destination is Senegal. You will need the tree bark to help you gain access." Prentice sat back on his hind legs and looked at her. "Access to what?" she asked. "To the wisdom of one of our greatest and wisest guardians. One of the oldest trees on the planet, a Baobab by the name of Takatifu. You may not need the map any further. I believe by the gift of bark you are probably being expected. You will need to cleanse first though; we're headed to Holy ground." Odara looked at him and said, "Thank you, Prentice, will you be cleansing with me?" Prentice laughed. "Cats are always clean, Ms. Odara. Always."

And so it begins

6
Looking for Answers

Odara and Prentice walked back to the main house. She needed to find a place on the property where she could summon her garden and do a body and spirit cleanse. Lisa was walking down the hall, and as she was passing them, she said, "There is an area adjacent to the house near the well that is completely hedged. Just some information for you in case you need some space with complete privacy. There is a door in the dining room that leads to it." Odara and Prentice looked at one another, and she heard Prentice in her mind saying, "Well, that takes care of that doesn't it." "Yes, it does," Odara responded aloud. Prentice raised his tail and headed towards the bedroom that he and Odara shared.

Odara immediately took stride to the dining room and went outside, using the door that she hadn't noticed when dining the previous Sunday. Once outside, she looked around and a smile began to form. The space was perfect for her to cleanse. The grass and ground surrounding her was neatly manicured with a small area in the center where a pergola was stationed.

Underneath the pergola was a sitting area

comprised of large pillows, a couple of ottomans, and a small table with candles on it. It reminded her of the altar in the center of her garden. Tall, thick hedges made up the perimeter of the area. You couldn't see out or into the area from either side of them. Odara walked to the center of the yard. She sat down on one of the pillows and began to embrace the stillness needed to center herself. First, she needed to summon her garden.

"For the purpose of cleansing, I summon the necessary components from my Sacred Garden. Be swift on the wings of Isis and deposit yourself for immediate bloom in this space. Once my purification and cleansing are complete, you will retreat and return from whence you came. You will present yourself in the area that I have outlined for you." Odara then rose to her feet and opened her palms. While turning in a full circle she chanted:

"Paladesima, with the fire that I was created from, I form a perimeter for placement of herbs from my Sacred Garden. I cleanse the soil that they will grace with the searing of the ground where it will remain until my cleansing has concluded. Sholakita, manisahira umbasanay!"

As she turned and chanted with her palms open, upturned streams of fire formed and shot into the ground surrounding her. When she had made a full circle, the streams stopped, and she looked around. In the area encircling her, the ground had been scorched and was smoldering. A 360-degree perimeter had been seared and purified by the fire from her palms. She took a seat again on one of the pillows and waited for her garden to transport to the space, then deposit and bloom for her cleansing.

In less than ten minutes, she felt the wind increase and saw the leaves on the hedges begin to move. The seared ground began to till on its own and she closed her eyes in anticipation. She could hear the whispers of the earth as it yielded for the deposits from her garden and welcomed her to do her work. When the wind settled and there was silence, she opened her eyes. Before she saw anything, she smelled the scent of fresh lavender carried by a slight breeze. She surveyed the cypher of herbs that surrounded her. Sage, Frankincense, Lavender, Rosemary, Hyssop, Tobacco, Mug Wort, and a new pleasant surprise of Sweetgrass. Everything was in full bloom and swayed back and forth in her direction, letting her know that they were here and ready to assist her. Without any further thought, she began the process.

"I command this space to be a chamber for spiritual cleansing." She held her palms out facing forward and assigned perimeters to the space until she had created a full sphere. "I give thanks for what has been entrusted to me and welcome the opportunity to be used again by something greater than me, for a purpose greater than mine. Immerse and bathe me now —I am fully present." She stretched out to lay down on the pillows in the center of the sphere. She closed her eyes and began to transition into a deep meditative state. While doing so, the temperature inside of the sphere began to increase steadily and the smell of protective herbs started to surround her. Within the next hour, the sphere had reached a temperature equivalent to a sauna. Her body was completely covered in droplets of sweat, and the offerings of sage from her sacred garden had consumed the air inside of it. She stretched out completely and allowed herself to be covered and bathed, purified and prepared. A few of hours later, she felt herself reaching what some people identify as the state of Nirvana. She would remain in this position, in the sphere until it released her – and when it did, she would literally be full of the fire that she was created from, and, the bathing process would transfer her into full warrior mode. She would be cleansed and prepared for interaction with anything. No human emotion or actions would be able to distract her.

When Odara awakened, it was a day later. The cool breeze from the early evening air awakened her. The sphere and the garden had released her. She sat straight up, feeling fully restored and ready to travel. She thanked the garden for what it had given her and headed back into the main house.

Upon entering the bedroom, she was staying in, Prentice stood up and stretched out. She immediately retrieved the piece of tree bark that was wrapped in the scrolled map. Carefully, she secured it in the satchel that was tied around her waist and said, "Time to go, Prentice." They were headed down the hallway when she noticed for the first time the beauty of the artwork that was gracing the walls. She slowed her pace and Prentice came to a complete stop. "I believe there is a gift here. Look closely, Odara." She looked at him and began to look with discerning eyes at every painting. In amazement, she watched as each piece came to life right before her.

The ocean waves in the lighthouse painting began to roll and she stepped back. The flowers in the painting of a field began to bloom and sway like they do in a springtime breeze. The next painting was the gift. A beautiful African girl was smiling, holding a basket full of coconuts *–No, mangos –No, Baobab fruit*! In the background of the picture was a massive Baobab. Odara stared at the tree and then looked directly into the eyes of the girl on the painting. The girl put the basket on top of her head and outstretched her hands to Odara. Prentice moved first. He turned himself into a walking staff in Odara's hand. She reached out for the girl's hands and was instantly transported to the path that the girl had been standing on. The path that led to one of the oldest trees on the planet where she would seek answers about the women who were disappearing, disrupting the rhythm of weaving the tapestries of life.

The young girl looked back at Odara from where she stood and said, "If you make it past the Gatekeepers, you will find the answers that you seek. Or at least a map to them. I bid you well." The girl then turned and walked away. She felt a strong vibration from the staff in her hand and heard Prentice's voice say, "Keep moving." Odara did an about face and started walking in the direction of the tree.

While walking towards the tree, she marveled at its size. As she drew nearer, it became more and more massive. There was a lot of folklore about Baobab trees and she was aware of all of it. None of it was rooted in truth, only speculation and imagination. The only thing that rang true about it was the name it was most commonly referred to: "The tree of life."

Culturally, the Baobab was shown much reverence, but in the spirit world, its significance was clear. The roots of the Baobab acted as receptors for everything happening throughout time on Earth. It was basically an ancient database that held the answers to the mysteries of everything on the planet. Odara needed access to that data to find out what was going on. She walked assuredly but slowly to the tree. When she stood directly in front of it and looked up, the branches towered stories above her. There were other people visiting the tree, some praying, some just admiring, and others seemingly just there to be there. She would have to wait until Sundown to initiate communication. So, she spread her cloak about her, sat down, and started eating some of the fruit in her satchel that she had brought with her. Looking at the staff, she asked Prentice if he was hungry. "Very rarely, my dear. I am able to walk centuries without a meal if necessary. When I indulge in certain environments, it's for aesthetics, not nutritional deprivation." Odara looked at the staff and laughed. "Lucky you, Sir. I have not reached that level of spirit warrior. I would love a pepperoni pizza with extra cheese right now." The staff vibrated slightly in amusement and said, "Oh, but you will, and when you do, even in human form your body will stay replenished. Hunger will no longer be a part of your experience." Odara finished her fruit and relaxed. She watched the people around the tree. She felt the presence of the power of the tree and she leaned back up against it to wait for the evening.

As the sun began to set, the tourists and local villagers began to disperse. The air was warm and still. Prentice had reclaimed his form as a cat and he was curled up in Odara's lap asleep. She had begun to drift in and out of a light sleep when she felt Prentice jump out of her lap. She was on her feet in one motion looking around. Prentice was on his feet and wasn't moving at all. She tuned in to focus her eyes in the direction that he was staring. The night sky had blanketed the landscape in darkness, so she had to focus. The tall grass that she was looking at was moving and beginning to part. There was no sense of heat in her palms, so she didn't feel the need to prepare for defense. A few moments later, the grass seemed to settle, and she looked down at Prentice with a question in her eyes. He sat back on his hind legs at full attention and didn't turn his head. When she looked up again, they were both looking at a pride of lions. But they weren't regular lions. These were spirit animals.

Majestic, beautiful, glowing, and massive in size. They were all staring directly at her.

The lion in the front of the pride had eyes that sparkled like the stars in the night sky. He roared and then took a step forward in Odara's direction. Prentice reacted immediately by assuming the form of one of the lions. Odara had no time to speak, move, or ask questions before he roared in response and stepped forward towards the pride. The other spirit lions took a step forward in unison and then sat down. At this point, the pride male who had stepped forward looked at Prentice and spoke in a language that Odara did not understand. Prentice responded in the same language and then stepped in front of Odara. The pride male took a step back and sat back on his hind legs. Still incredibly massive and beautiful with a strong but softened tone, he addressed Odara. "We are the Gatekeepers of this tree of life. We understand that you seek some of the knowledge and wisdom that is rooted here. We also understand that you are not of this Earth, even though you are physically presented as so. Unfortunately for you, we were not informed that a visitor would arrive on such a quest. Because of this, you will only be granted access if you can present the key that will prove to us that you are worthy of access. If you do not have a key, the portal to access the wisdom of the tree will be sealed, and you will be expelled from this premise. Do you have a key?" Odara looked into the eyes of the spirit lion. Feeling defeated and bewildered, she lowered her head to answer, "I was not given a key, only a map of this country and this piece of bark." She untied her satchel and pulled the bark out for him to see. When she did, the bark in her hand doubled in size then quivered in her hand. The pride male took two steps back and sat down. Never taking his eyes off Odara, he spoke again, "The gift you were given is the key that you will need. When you place that bark in the spot that it is missing on the tree, you will be granted access into the hollow, and there, you will be able to ask the questions that you need answers to." When he finished speaking, the entire pride began to spread out around the tree. As she and Prentice watched, they formed a full circle around its entire circumference and looked up at the tree. Their presence provided enough illumination for Odara to see the tree clearly. She stared up at it and processed the magnitude of it. She would have to canvas the whole tree to find the spot of missing bark that matched the shape of the piece that she held.

"In the interest of time, allow me to assist you, please." Prentice then took the form of bird. Odara made her ascent while Prentice began to circle the tree in flight. They scoured every inch, finding missing pieces but none that were the shape of the bark that Odara had in her possession. The spirit pride sat patiently, watching them as they searched. The job of the pride now was to maintain watch over the tree until Odara had gained access. They would not leave until she was safely inside. In the event that anything or anyone in human or spirit form besides Odara tried to enter with her, they would destroy it. Odara was halfway up the tree when she saw what she was looking for. She called out to Prentice to make him aware, and he was by her side in the blink of an eye.

Odara placed the bark in the spot that it appeared to have originated from, and it fit perfectly. The wind swooped and Prentice returned to the base of the tree in his original form so that could he watch. The branches of the tree began to extend themselves downward and inward in Odara's direction. She heard the creaking sound of old wooden doors opening and closing as the branches began to form a stairwell for her. She looked down after taking them upward and realized that she was at the very top of this enormous tree. The center of the tree opened, and the stairwell then began to lower with her standing on it. When it stopped, she stepped off the stairwell and stood looking around her. She was inside the hollow of the Baobab, standing in a large chamber that was ancient beyond her recognition.

Odara was awestruck. She had traveled for centuries through many planes and dimensions, back and forth through thousands of time periods, but she had never been anywhere that wasn't in the spirit realm that felt like this. She could feel the strength of the tree, the wisdom coursing through it, and even the Earth she stood on inside of the hollow felt uniquely wonderous. She was humbled. The walls were intricately covered with stories in languages of cultures from all over the world. There were pillars of fossilized wood in between each section covered with lush green moss, and amid some of the stories were small crystal formations that seemed to indicate an ending or signify some sort of change in direction. The stories started at the base of the tree and continued upward as far as she could see. The sight of it all was incredulous.

Odara sat on the ground inside of the tree. Her connection with the earth was intensified here. She could feel the planet welcoming her. She closed her eyes in gratitude for this experience, and then she heard the sound of movement. She opened her eyes, and small, thin tree roots were beginning to break through the ground in front of a section of one of the walls. They began to spread out and cover that section, slowly creeping upward. She marveled as the roots kept extending and expanding as they traveled, and she noticed that the words written in what she believed to be Sanskrit in that section appeared to be "moving." She took a deep breath and tears began to flow; she was witnessing the tree add to its recordings. She was so engrossed in what she was seeing that she didn't notice the beginning of the ground opening up, right in front of where she sat.

Odara repositioned herself so that she could continue to watch the roots at work. She then heard the sound of something breaking through the earth. It wasn't an unfamiliar sound; she had heard it before while watching her Sacred Garden come to life. Seeing something emerge from the earth wasn't foreign to her either. She had seen many fruits of the earth come to life right before her eyes. She had even traveled to a plane and time where the hills and trees were alive. None of that however, prepared her for what was rising from the ground. Thousands of tiny roots were breaking through the earth and intertwining themselves, working their way up.

They were forming into the shape of a woman. She dropped her gaze so as not to stare disrespectfully during the formation process. A voice that sounded like many voices in one said, "You need not look away." Odara returned her gaze to watch and saw that the roots were now carefully sculpting arms and hands after having completed the rest of a full body. She looked at what had become a very striking face. Small leaves began to sprout and form a long tunic and before she knew it, the roots had tightly woven themselves into a mesmerizing, statuesque woman who now stood in front of Odara. With kindness in her eyes, the woman said, "Welcome warrior for good, Odara of the second sentry from the spirit realm of the heavens where the Sacred Council presides. My name is one to be never written nor spoken in the languages that you speak. For the purpose of our meeting, you may call me Ukweli."

Odara got on her knees and bowed to her. She then sat back down on the ground. Ukweli sat down on the ground facing Odara and spoke. "I appreciate the reverence, but it is not necessary. Anyone who is not worthy of my presence does not make it past the Gatekeepers, sometimes even with a key. I hope they didn't frighten you – of course they didn't, even with the magnitude of their size, you wouldn't be frightened by anything in spirit form. I understand that you are quite exceptional – "chosen," I believe would be the word for you. Forgive me if I ramble. I'm only able to communicate through spoken word every few hundred years and I enjoy it. That would make you Odara, the twentieth person in six thousand years that I've spoken to. Can you imagine that? To have all of the access that I have, to know what I know and only have the opportunity to share selected information twenty times. I'm sure you can't. You probably talk to twenty people a week. But I'm never bored, you know. The earth is constantly downloading information that I must record. Enough of that now, what do you seek to know, Odara of the second sentry?"

Odara told Ukweli about the weavers and what their purpose was. She shared what Intisar had shared with her and told her about witnessing the holes grow and spread. She told her about what she saw on the land at her Chateau in France. She then concluded with her plight. "I need to know where the women are and who or what is behind the disappearances? Once I know that, I believe I will know how to put an end to it." Ukweli sat motionless for a moment and then she rose. Walking towards one of the walls, she turned to Odara and said, "I have questions that will require short answers, preferably a yes or no answer when possible. When I stop asking questions, you will remain seated and silent until I take a seat beside you again, do you understand?" "Yes," Odara replied. "First, these weavers, this Intisar, what time and place does she exist in?" Second, who delivers her threads to her? Third, the missing women, what time and place did they exist in? Fourth, when you were told of their plight, did you feel fear or sorrow? Fifth, do you believe that you can put a definite end to the disruption? Sixth, are you aware that the battle you may be headed into could possibly be the hardest that you've ever encountered? And lastly, do you give me your word, Odara of the Second Sentry, that nothing you encounter here will ever be shared once you leave this chamber?

Odara stood up and began to answer the questions. "Intisar resides on a Caribbean island that exists during the mid-1800s. Her threads are delivered to her by a personification of God. The missing women existed in the United States of America, the time of the disruption is between 2016-2019. I felt fear and sorrow. Yes, Yes, and Yes." Ukweli had listened intently and was watching Odara as she spoke. She told her to sit down. "This will not be as simple as I had anticipated. I will provide you as much information that I can gather from the walls."

Ukwlei walked alongside the inner walls of the trees looking upward, scanning for what she needed. With every step she took, the walls lit up and the stories revolved. When she got to a certain section, she stopped and placed her hands on the wall. She closed her eyes as the form of body began to unravel and the roots that she was made up of began to spread out and canvas the walls. As she worked her way up the wall, she would pause occasionally. Odara waited patiently, silently praying and dreading what the information could possibly disclose. After some time had passed, the form of Ukweli was no longer discernable. All she could see were roots moving in several directions at one time. Odara dozed off and fell asleep. She was awakened by the sound of Ukweli's voice.

"I have information for you, Odara of the second sentry." Ukweli had reassumed the stately form of a female and was sitting in front of Odara on the ground again. She waited for Odara to sit up and be fully present before she began to speak. "In answer to the questions that you asked, I have found that none of these women were connected through physical or spiritual ties. There are dead ends and no information on who they were becoming or how they would've impacted the world. I have names and places and the events that led up to their disappearances but nothing more. To add to this lack of information, I do not have a trace of anything Earthly being responsible for their situations. I am only able to provide you with the name of someone who can take you to another sacred place where the wisdom of the sky meets the earth. Her name is Kelly. In order to get to her, you need listen for the sound of a baby crying. When you hear it, you will know that you are being summoned because the cry of this child will come on the wings of the wind. I am sorry that with the wealth of information here, I am unable to provide more."

Odara thanked Ukweli and stayed in the position that she was in, processing what she had been told. This was getting uglier and uglier. If whomever or whatever was responsible for the disappearances wasn't of the earth, what kind of evil entity was wreaking havoc by stealing lives? She was still thinking about it when Ukweli stood and said, "Your task is great, Odara of the second sentry. I hope that should I see you again, I can be of more assistance." Ukweli crossed her arms over her chest and stood still. Odara did not move as the roots had intertwined to form Ukweli began to move in reverse, undoing what they had done to form her. The earth began to open up again, and as the roots released her form, they descended back into the ground. Odara stood and the stairwell began to lower in her direction. She took the first few steps and it lifted her to the top of the tree. It then lowered her on the outside of it to the ground at the base of the tree, where Prentice was waiting and the Gatekeepers were still sitting at attention. Once she set foot on the ground, the Gatekeepers vanished. Prentice waited for Odara to speak or move. She moved, and in one sweeping gesture, she gathered him in her arms and spoke to the wind, "Ascend now, back to the Augustin house."

When Odara and Prentice landed at the Augustin house, they landed in the formal dining room. Several days had passed and the family was just about to partake in the only meal that they shared together once a week, Sunday dinner. No one seemed surprised or startled when Odara appeared out of nowhere near the dinner table with Prentice in her arms. Lisa came out of the kitchen with a small bowl of food and sat it on the floor near the fireplace for Prentice. Odara saw that a place had been set for her and she took her seat. The Augustin women were chattering and laughing amongst themselves. All of them except for Intisar.

Dressed in an astonishing yellow and orange long-sleeved brocade dress, fitted at the bodice with a full flowing skirt and wearing a crown of fresh red flowers in her hair, she looked like one of the paintings on the wall at the Louvre. Intisar asked her if she had received any help. Odara replied yes, and that she was given enough to head in the right direction. "I was hoping that the light that kept trying to surface in my tapestry over the last few days was you making progress." Intisar picked up her fork and began to eat her dinner. Odara followed suit and enjoyed the multiple varieties of dishes on the table. When dinner was over, Prentice came to her side and said, "You need rest. Your spirit is strong, but the body needs to replenish." He turned and started walking out of the dining room.

Odara placed her napkin on the table and proceeded to follow him to the bedroom that they were sharing to get some sleep. As they made their way down the hallway that led to the room, Odara slowed to look again at the pictures on the walls in the hallway. They were still there, although there was no movement in them and nothing that made them stand out. When she got to the space that held the picture of the Senegalese girl with the Baobab fruit, there had been a change. The girl was no longer in the picture. It was now a painting of a large Baobab with a pride of lions sitting in a nearby field.

When she stepped closer to look at the details, the Pride male turned to face her. With sparkling eyes, he nodded his head and then resumed his position. Odara returned the nod and said thank you before entering the bedroom with Prentice to get some much-needed sleep.

Nothing is as it seems

7
Discovery

Odara had expended so much spiritual energy through her travel and experiences in the previous week that her physical body was exhausted. She woke up from sleeping, thinking that she had just slept through the night. Prentice sitting on the edge of the bed staring at her. She sat up in the bed and greeted him. “Good morning, Prentice.” “Good evening, actually, Ms. Odara, I allowed you to remain asleep because we still have much to do, and I feeling that a powerful battle requiring transference of energies will be involved. You are probably not accustomed to being so tired from traveling. In case you didn’t know, not only did you travel through a portal to another place and time, but you also entered another dimension once you entered the hollow of the Baobab. That my dear, is a lot for anyone who is operating in a physical body. I will need some fire from you for the next leg of our assignment. If you open your palm for me, it will present itself.” Prentice jumped off the bed and walked to the side of the bed where Odara was sitting. He arched his back and looked up towards the ceiling. Odara heard wind chimes, and Prentice stood before her as a Shaman Priest.

Standing over six feet tall, he towered above her and was dressed in ceremonial clothing; his presence was electrifying. He was chanting in some sort of Native Indian language as he passed his hands in the air over her body. She began to feel strength flood through her body; a quickening in her muscles and power in her spirit. Without question, she closed her eyes and allowed him to finish what he was doing. When he ceased from chanting, he told her to stand and stretch out her palms.

Odara got out of the bed and stood before him. She felt formidable. Like he had removed her exhaustion and replenished her from head to toe. She extended her palms to him and instantly the embers that were placed in her palms to create her call appeared, glowing fiercely and slightly aflame. Prentice placed his palms over hers and the room shook. She saw the clouds rolling in large waves through the open curtain on the window. Then she heard the drums. The ancestral drums that sounded through the air when her body was being formed for the first time. She felt the fire in her coursing through her veins. She closed her eyes and felt herself going into a trance. They stood with their palms locked until the drumming stopped. Prentice released her hands and instantaneously resumed his form as a cat. Odara was becoming more and more fascinated by him with every experience. At that moment, what she understood for sure without question was that he was extremely powerful and there to aid and protect her. She was grateful for his presence. The Sacred Council had outdone themselves when they gifted her with him.

Prentice walked back over to the pillow that was provided for him to sleep on and began to stretch and yawn. Odara was tickled watching him do what cats do, knowing that he was an indescribable force to reckon with. She noticed that a cart had been brought into the room. She didn't know if it had been delivered throughout the course of the day or while she was in a trance transferring fire from her body to Prentice. However, she did know that there was food on it and that she was famished. She removed the linen that covered the cart and there was a bowl of steaming hot broth, fresh bread, and a salad fit for a king, loaded with fresh vegetables. There was a small carafe of wine and a coffee pot along with all the necessary utensils to enjoy her meal.

She ate slowly and allowed herself to enjoy the food. The wine was a perfect red blend and the coffee was the perfect after dinner accompaniment. After eating, she walked over to the basin and filled it with water from the pitcher placed on the stand next to it. She immersed one of her hands to heat the water and when it was hot enough, she removed her hand and began to wash herself with the wonderful smelling homemade soap on the table. After scrubbing herself from head to toe, she sat down on the bed and thought about what she had learned from Ukweli. A child's cry. That's what would come to her. She was ready for whatever it was. She was very disturbed by what Intisar had shared with her. It was almost painful. She decided that she would walk the grounds of the Augustin family home and go meditate under the Magnolia in the front yard. The still of the night would make for a peaceful setting.

Odara slipped into a white linen hooded dress with long sleeves, and as an afterthought, she secured her satchel around her waist. *Just in case*, she thought. When she opened the door to exit the room, Prentice looked at her and was afoot in one jump. They headed down the hall, out of the house, and into the yard. She decided that she would meditate before taking her walk. They strolled towards the Magnolia tree that was in full bloom. The smell of the flowers and the sight of them, even in the night, was beautiful. She was pleased to see that the bench under the tree once again, had been set up to accommodate her. She made a mental note that Lisa had not missed a beat in anticipating her needs from the moment that she had arrived. She sat on the bench and folded her legs underneath her. As soon as she had relaxed completely, she saw the flame in the lantern begin to grow as if being fanned-- but there was no breeze. No sooner than she noticed the flame, her palms began to heat up. She looked up at the sky and saw a lone bird in flight. It circled in the night sky and then took a dive headed in their direction.

Odara and Prentice were on their feet at the sight of the bird flying towards them. The temperature in her palms was increasing but not with a sense of danger, more of a call to action. When the bird landed on the ground a few feet away from them, she saw that it was an owl. A rather large, all white, beautiful owl. The bird looked at them and then scratched the ground with his feet. He took a couple of steps and continued to scratch at the ground until he had drawn a full line about five feet across. He then stopped and stared at them. He outstretched his wings, and as they spread out, streams of glittering light began to shoot upward from the line he had drawn. He took two steps towards Odara and Prentice and took off in flight. Odara turned in the direction that he had flown away but there was no trace of him. She looked at the light coming from the ground with the appearance of stars floating in it. The owl had delivered the doorway to a portal, but she had received instructions to listen for the sound of a baby and there was none. Noticing that Prentice hadn't moved or said a word, she didn't move either. Instead, she closed her eyes to meditate.

As she began to transfer into a heavy meditational state about thirty minutes later, she thought she heard a whimper. She opened her eyes and saw that Prentice was comfortably curled up in sleep position. She closed her eyes and refocused on the clearing of her mind. A few minutes passed and there was another sound that broke her concentration. This time, it was discernable and absolute; the sound of a baby crying. Prentice stood at attention. She wasn't sure if he could hear it too, but he knew that something was happening. They both looked at the doorway to the portal and the light that was flickering, and glistening had intensified. Prentice jumped onto Odara's shoulder and draped himself as a shawl. Odara walked to the doorway, crossed her arms over her chest, and walked through it.

Samara had left the workshop to go and try to engage with Odara. She was both delighted and intrigued by her. Always barefoot, Samara loved the feel of the ground underneath her feet as she walked towards the main house. Upon entering, she saw Odara and Prentice walking out of the front door. She was just as mesmerized by Prentice as she was Odara. The fact that he acknowledged her telepathic greeting upon his arrival only enhanced her curiosity about his assignment with Odara. Samara wasn't sure why or how she knew the things that she knew. She just knew that her ability to see, hear, and feel things was beyond the capacity of her sisters, even though they were gifted too. She tried to get Odara and Prentices' attention before they walked out of the front door, but they were moving too quickly. Samara walked to the large, heavily draped window to see what they were doing. She peered through a small opening in the drapes and saw that Odara and Prentice were both preoccupied, looking upward at something in the sky. Samara almost squealed aloud when a ridiculously enormous and beautiful owl dropped down and began scratching at the ground. Odara turned her head towards the house and Samara stepped back from the drapery.

Maybe she wasn't supposed to see what they were doing. She took a deep breath and her curiosity got the best of her. Samara stepped forward and looked through the opening in the drapes again. Her mouth dropped open as she watched Prentice *transform* himself into a shawl that Odara draped across her shoulders and then – they stepped through an *illuminated doorway* and were gone! Samara was amazed and thrilled. She had memories of places she'd never been in her life. At times, she would get urges to get up from her loom and see if she could transport herself to another place. The lives and stories that she recorded through weaving her tapestries kept her in a state of constant wonder. She had always felt that her life couldn't possibly be to just weave the stories of others until she died. Her heart was beating rapidly. Samara decided that before Odara left, she would ask her about what exactly it is that she does, and who did she need to talk to in order to get that job.

Odara had stepped through the portal and now she was in a large park. She looked around and saw hundreds of people. A lot of them were wearing pink. She took a moment to acquaint herself with her surroundings. There was a woman on a large stage singing and her voice was magical. She continued to scan and saw the banners throughout the park bearing the pink ribbon, which was the identifier for breast cancer awareness. She could no longer hear the baby crying, so she was going to be still until she received a sign of what to do next. She was taking in the energy of the celebration and the people in attendance. The power and strength of the women who were obviously survivors of breast cancer and their supporters was almost tangible. It filled her human side with warmth and pride. The woman on the stage singing had finished, and the MC for the event was trying to get the crowd ready for the next performer. She described numerous contributions, awards, and accolades – giving high praise to the talent of the next performer. Odara's attention was mobilized when she said, "Without further ado, please welcome the phenomenal spoken word queen that we all know and love. She goes by the artist name of Kellygirl!" *Kelly*. That was the name of the person who would take her where she needed to go for possible answers that Ukweli couldn't provide. She moved forward and began to make her way through the crowd while they cheered and applauded Kelly as she graced the stage. By the time the crowd was calm enough for her to speak, Odara was only two rows away from the front of the stage.

Kelly was an astonishingly beautiful, graceful young woman. Dark cocoa-colored skin, eyes that sparkled, and regal in her stature. Odara liked her already. Kelly had on a long flowing pink strapless dress that literally illuminated against her skin. What assured Odara that this was the Kelly that she was to connect with was the fact that Kelly had come on stage with a beautiful baby boy strapped to her body in a harness. She could see the baby staring up into his mother's face with his head on her chest; he was in absolute love and peace with her. Odara was smitten. Kelly looked out into the crowd and smiled. She began with, "Thank you for the love. I am honored. I won't bore you with the mushy sentiments, I promise. You know why I'm here, let's get to it!" The crowd went crazy and she took a step away from the microphone. When she stepped back to it, the crowd hushed, and she began her spoken word piece. Kelly was fire! All power as she delivered her piece on survival being a mindset. She spit her piece out with confidence and grace. Odara was thrilled. This Sista was bad to the bone. As Kelly finished her piece, she looked down at the front of the stage and they made eye contact. Kelly winked at her, finished her piece, and announced where she would be stationed for photos and autographs of her book. The audience screamed, whistled, and clapped while chanting her name. She then floated off the stage like a butterfly.

Odara gave Kelly a few minutes to meet and greet with her fans before she walked over to the booth where she was sitting. As she was approaching, Kelly stood up and told the other women in her booth to take over because she would have to head home to get her son Apollo out of the warm air. Kelly came from behind the booth with arms extended. Pleasantly surprised, Odara exchanged a hug with her and then stepped back. Kelly was more stunning face to face than she was onstage. She radiated with kindness but there was a fierce undercurrent that told Odara she was not to be underestimated in any capacity. Kelly leaned forward and spoke quickly and softly, "We need to move now.

Come with me, and I will take you where you need to be. And please, don't be alarmed by what I know of you. My son, Apollo is gifted in many ways, and even though he is an infant, he tells me everything that he hears. If you combine that with the gifts I was blessed with and what I have been entrusted with, we're a pretty powerful team." Odara looked at Apollo who had the face of an angel. He was sleeping peacefully against his mother's chest in the midst of all the festival commotion. "Follow me," Kelly said as she began to almost glide through the crowds of people. Odara did as she said and kept pace with her. Prentice was still resting on her shoulders as a shawl. They got into a car and Odara rode in silence while Kelly hummed to the music from the CD playing.

Twenty minutes later, Kelly pulled up to a mid-sized home with an immaculately manicured yard. She got out and took Apollo out of his car seat. Once she had her son in her arms, she said, “Your companion is welcome as well.” Prentice took form and hopped to the ground. Kelly almost squealed. “I didn’t know it was a cat.” Prentice dropped his head, and Kelly said, “No, I didn’t mean it that way. I love cats and he is beautiful. I’m certain that his presence as your companion means he is really much more than what meets the eye.” *You have no idea*, Odara thought. Prentice looked up at her and smirked, and they followed Kelly into her home.

Kelly’s home was as warm and inviting as she was. There were rich earth tones in every room with bright pops of color to accent everything. She invited Odara to have a seat and told her she would be right back. Odara sat down on the sofa and Prentice sat at her feet. In what couldn’t have been more than ten minutes, Kelly popped back into the living room. She had changed into a pair of jeans and hiking boots, pulled her hair back into a ponytail, and Apollo was bundled quite nicely in a yellow blanket. Kelly walked over to her fireplace and reached for her clock. She wound the minute hand back and forth, stopping at specific numbers, the same way someone would operate a safe combination. When she stopped, the second hand circled twice and stopped on 12. Two of the bricks in the fireplace pushed forward. Kelly pulled them out and retrieved a large black book. She replaced the bricks and said, "Let's go." Odara and Prentice followed her back outside to the car. Once in motion, Kelly spoke to her. "We have about an hour's ride and then we'll have to pull off the main road. Once we get to the clearing, we'll have to get out and walk. I really hope that I can help you because this world, this country, is in trouble. I don't know everything about you, but I know enough to know that you may be the key to setting some things straight. That's comforting to me because when Apollo has dreams and wakes up upset or afraid, it's not because he's hungry or needs to be changed, it's because something ugly is going on in the world that needs to be changed. When he is afraid, so am I, because he is frightened by very little. He told me that you were coming and that you would help. I hope that he's right. I find myself in tears almost every time I open that book and must add another name to it. It's traumatizing to see the stories on the news or social media and then there's nothing. No follow up, no mention of investigations or attempts to solve anything. Just a story about another missing Black woman and then everything continues as if nothing has happened."

Odara took in what she was saying then asked her, "What's in the book and where did you get it?" Kelly told her that the book appeared on her desk at work one day in a box. There were hundreds of small sheets of paper with names and dates on them in the box with the book. When she opened the book, there was a note that said for her to record every name and date that is given to her. She didn't even know at the time what the names meant or who they belonged to. After that, every so often she would find a small piece of paper on the ground, in her mailbox, in her purse etc., and she would add the name and date to the book. She said she doesn't know where the book came from, but one day, she opened it and there were instructions for her to go where she was taking Odara. Odara listened to Kelly without interrupting. Kelly went on to say that none of it was strange to her and that she was never fearful or questionable about any of it. She had a son who had been named after a God and he was specially gifted, so nothing else was surprising to her anymore. She felt that her job was to be obedient. If something greater than her felt that she was worthy of what she had been entrusted with then she would do whatever she was asked if her family was not in danger.

Kelly took a turn from the main highway, and they were now on a dirt road passing fields and lots of trees. As the landscape began to widen,

Odara rolled the window down for fresh air and enjoyed the beauty of undeveloped land. She saw mountains and hills further out and smiled. Not too much longer, Kelly pulled her car over next to a large Juniper tree and parked it. "We have to walk from here.," Kelly said as she parked and got out to get Apollo. Odara and Prentice exited the vehicle and waited for Kelly. After she had strapped Apollo to her chest in the baby harness, Kelly motioned for them to follow her.

They started walking away from the car. It was an easy walk at first, and then the terrain began to increase in incline. As they walked, the trees in the landscape began to thin out and they were walking through fields of wild grass. After thirty minutes had passed, Odara was wondering how much longer they would need to walk. She could offer to transport them if it was going to take a lot longer. While she was pondering to offer her assistance, Kelly stopped walking near the foot of the first hill they had neared. Odara and Prentice looked up and saw that the hills were all connected and seemed to line up in rows. They were breathtaking. Kelly began to remove the harness and asked Odara to hold her son. Odara obliged, thinking that this must be a spot for them to rest for a moment. When she took Apollo in her arms, he opened his arms and embraced her. She had a moment where she thought about the fact that she would never have a child of her own to hold and then she heard the words, “You don’t know that.” She looked into Apollo’s little face and he was gurgling and smiling up at her. “You can speak to me?” she asked. “Of course I can. I can do a lot of things, but I must introduce them slowly to my parents. They don’t know who I am yet. Mommy is starting to figure it out though.” Odara looked into his eyes to search. She saw the skies and the heavens and then the sun reflecting in them. Apollo was a Sun baby. His name was no coincidence. All over the world there were children whose birth had been marked by the sun or the moon. These bright-eyed children were gifts from the universe, specifically chosen to bring light and harmony into the lives of everyone in the world around them. Some of them, like Apollo, were blessed with extra capabilities like clairvoyance, telepathy, and the gift of conjure. She wrapped her arms around him and closed her eyes to share with him. They communicated much in silence and she felt the warmth of the sun flowing from him to her. She released the conversation and he giggled. Kelly was kneeling in front of the hill. Odara was about to ask if she should transport them further when

Kelly looked up at her and gave her the hush sign.

Prentice sat at Odara's feet with a look of wonder. *This is going to be good*, Odara thought, if even Prentice is anticipating what's next. Kelly stretched her body forward and placed her palms on the ground at the base of the hill.

"We beseech the assistance of the women who rest, may we be granted entrance to your residence to assist us in a quest for knowledge that will impact the madness that is attacking us. I humbly ask for favor in your sight."

Kelly stopped speaking and stood up. She took Apollo back into her arms and stepped closer to Odara. As quickly as she did, a rumbling began. It increased in volume and then ceased. The grass on the hillside started blowing in a non-existent wind and the earth opened on the side of the hill facing them. They walked to the opening and stepped inside. Once they were all inside, it closed quickly behind them. Kelly started walking further into the space. Odara followed with Prentice on her heels. The space opened into an enormous room. Odara saw the walls and dropped to her knees. Prentice assumed the form of a woman and did the same. Thousands of women were carved into the walls of the hill.

Then they all began to speak at once, some asking questions, some giving information, some singing, some laughing, and some crying. It was incredible. Odara didn't know if Kelly knew what she had been gifted with by being entrusted with access to these women. These women were the caretakers of stories of unfulfilled destinies. Odara had only heard of them. Even the Sacred Council was never certain where they resided. And they were right here. Living in the walls of a hill somewhere in Northern California in the year 2019. Odara was humbled and outdone.

While Odara and Prentice were on their faces waiting for permission to speak, all the voices went silent and Odara heard a smooth, silky voice say, "What may we assist you with today, Daughter Kelly?" Kelly explained why they were there and sat down holding Apollo. The same voice then addressed Odara, "The respect you've shown is duly noted. Please stand and step forward, Odara." She did as she was told and then the voice said loudly, "Let Odara see!" The carvings in the walls began to move and assimilate into lines of women, they looked like an army. As they repositioned themselves, Odara watched in amazement. Once a section of the wall was completely in order, the carvings stepped forward out of the wall and then they moved aside. They looked like a battalion of stone female soldiers standing massively to one side lined up. "See now, Odara," the voice said.

Odara looked at the wall where the carvings had abdicated their positions. She felt her heart drop in her chest when her eyes focused. The wall had become a stone movie screen and on it were multiple scenes scrolling. Abduction, rape, murder, trafficking, suicide, and organ harvesting. Thousands of frightening, sad, and horrific scenes and faces of women crying out, begging for help, begging for release, praying, fighting in defense, names, dates, times, places, and then a loud wail of desperation and despair.

The wall went blank, and the carvings stepped forward, reassumed their original positions, and merged back into it. Winded and disgusted, Odara did not move a muscle. Kelly appeared at her side and handed her the Black book. "Now you know what has happened. I hope that you can do something to prevent it from increasing. I hope that you can put a stop to it for all time. I am filled with hope, because I believe in the greater good." Odara hugged Kelly with tears streaming down her face and Kelly held her for a moment. When they stepped away from one another, Kelly asked the Hill to release them with a return.

The next thing Odara knew, they were standing next to Kelly's car by the Juniper. They got into the car, and Kelly took a deep breath and exhaled. A tear rolled down her cheek. “My apologies, it affects me the same every time I add a name. What I saw today for the first time were the faces of my girlfriends, my mother, my friend’s daughters, my cousins, aunts, and even my own. It could be any of us at any given moment. All of these women, they’re a part of us, of all Black women. So much going on. I am already dreading teaching my son how to survive a traffic stop. I’m already worried about the children walking down the street alone on their way to school or a teenage girl waiting alone at a bus stop. I’m already worried about if the world will even be existent long enough for my son’s children to have children. It’s all so much, and now whenever I see other women, especially Black women, I’ll be praying that they make it home safely. That they won’t disappear without a trace and see nothing being done about it.

No mass media coverage, no ongoing investigations, no en masse events supporting our safety and their return. I’ll be looking over my shoulder everywhere I go. I believe that whatever is happening is under the direction of something purely evil.” Odara took her hand and said nothing. She felt the truthful sting of everything that Kelly had said. They sat for a few minutes, and Odara looked into the back seat at

Apollo who was dozing off and Prentice who was curled in the seat staring at her. "You may be able to ask them yourself," he said. "Every element of the earth is directly connected to you.

Do not be discouraged, access your allies. There are many." When the message from Prentice came to her from the back seat, she heard the crashing sound of waves. Kelly started driving and asked her, "Where shall I take you?" Odara looking out of the window at the upcoming highway replied, "To the nearest ocean."

No stone unturned

8
Recovery

Back at the Augustin home, it was 5 a.m. and the Augustin women were having their morning tea. Samara was extremely high spirited and excited. She chattered on extensively about random subjects. Zora was listening to her youngest sibling intently. When Samara finally took a moment to exhale and allow someone else to speak, Zora addressed her sisters. "Has anyone noticed anything awry with their work lately?" Intisar, alarmed, responded immediately with, "Why do you ask?" Zora, who was the most modest and the mildest in temperament of the Augustin women, responded with, "I asked you all a question?" There was an obvious discomfort in the room. They had never ever discussed their tapestries, the stories they recorded, or their sentiments for as long as they had been weaving. Zora was transparently troubled by something, and she wanted to know if anyone else was. The only person to respond again was Intisar. "I've had some discrepancies in my fabric, holes to be specific. What makes it troubling is that they appear out of nowhere, sometimes days after I've finished a section. I can feel the separation from the pattern as strongly as I feel the disruption in the lives of the people I'm weaving about. It's very daunting.

I'm hoping that Odara can provide some assistance to end these disruptions." Zora took a sip of her tea and wondered if she was treading dangerous ground with her line of questioning. She was carrying some angst about her own tapestries, and she wasn't certain if the next question she needed to ask violated the sanctity of what they do. She decided to ask anyway.

"Intisar, what realm are you assigned to? I ask because I'm wondering if what you're assigned to has an impact on what I'm assigned to record. I haven't seen any holes, but my threads seem to tangle and knot up, sometimes even break, and I have to stop and try to repair them as I work. Even though that is something that has never happened until recently, that's not the strange part. The strange, or rather puzzling part is that after I repair them, and when I look back over my day's work, the knots, tangles, and broken threads have reappeared." Intisar looked at her sister Zora, the peacemaker, the affirmer, the voice of reason for the Augustin women. She took a deep breath and answered her. "The 8th realm, planet Earth, currently the year 2019 is what I am recording. The common denominator with my holes is African American women and girls." Obviously shaken, Zora set her tea down. All of the Augustin women looked at Intisar and then at Zora. Aunt Ethel B, who was sitting next to Zora, took Zora's hand in hers and asked, "What are you assigned to, Zora?" Zora was instantly comforted by the touch of her aunt's hand and the concern and love in her voice. She looked in her eyes and said, "Earth, The 9th realm, the doorways to life or eternity, destiny or fate. Currently the knots and breaks have appeared where a child is at the point of conception, or where there is a life changing event. All of the disruptions have been African American children." Aunt Ethel B held Zora's hand tightly and said nothing. Intisar understood immediately the connection. Her other sisters hadn't spoken but they too looked concerned and appeared to be holding back for now. She closed her eyes for a moment and said a silent prayer for Odara to be successful. This was turning out to be much more than she thought.

Odara sensed something in her spirit. She closed her eyes and saw the Augustin women having their morning tea. There seemed to be some sadness and surprise in the air. She focused in, and the faces of Intisar and Zora revealed pain, question, and uncertainty. She sent Intisar a message, "*I will do what I promised to do.*"

Then she opened her eyes and began to look around. The ride to the ocean was beautiful.

Odara gave silent thanks and acknowledgements to all of the hills, mountains, and trees that were in sight as they passed by them. Fully aware that in each of them was life and a history that people of this dimension and time would never know, outside of fantasy movies and books. Kelly was quiet during the drive. Apollo, who giggled and held baby conversation with himself most of the ride had fallen into a deep sleep. Prentice was also taking advantage of the opportunity to rest. Odara couldn't rest. The human part of her was angry, restless, hurt, and disgusted. The spiritual warrior in her was prepared to forfeit her body if necessary, to put an end to whoever/whatever was responsible for the disappearances of 64,000 African American women in the United States of America.

She cringed from the thought that there were probably more that weren't documented or reported. She noted to herself that the year she was in was 2019, and a lot of things seemed out of order. The energy in the air was chaotic, full of desperation, and people were lacking in empathy, basic kindness, and integrity. She had taken in enough of the air around her to feel it all, and it did not feel good. Wondering what went wrong and where, Odara sat looking out of the window. She knew that the ocean, the sea, was a very powerful place to get answers. She was certain that the answers from the source that all life depends on would give her what she needed.

After a two-hour ride, Odara smiled when the view from the window began to show a coastline. Within minutes of it coming into full view, Kelly turned to exit the highway and drove up a road that led to a parking area. Once parked, Odara turned to Kelly and said, "I know this isn't the last time that we will see one another. I have a feeling that Apollo and I have some unfinished business. Thank you for everything, Ms. Kelly. Farewell and blessings to you." Kelly got out of the car and gave her a hug. "Thank you, Odara, for the work that you do. My prayer is that when you've done what you came to do, I will never receive another name to record anywhere.

Apollo and I will be looking forward to whenever our paths cross again." As she got back into the car and Prentice took her place by Odara's side, Apollo had awakened and turned his head to look out the window at her. He smiled and his eyes sparkled. Apollo sent Odara a silent message. "The next time I see you, I will be standing by your side, and it will be a joyous occasion." Prentice jumped into the air and did a full flip. Apollo squealed with laughter. Odara and Prentice turned and began walking down the path towards the beachfront where the sun was rapidly setting.

The sight of the ocean with the sun setting on the water was stunning and powerful. Bluish-green waves softly rolled and subsided from the shore while the sun reflected gold, pink, and purple waves in the distance as it made its descent. Odara looked out into the ocean and was humbled by the magnitude of water and its power. "I respect you!" she said aloud. What she needed to do there was to be done at night by the light of the moon and there were still a few people walking the beach. Prentice tugged at her skirt and beckoned her to sit. She sat down in lotus position and Prentice climbed into her lap. She took a deep breath and freed her mind of all thought. Now all she had to do was wait for the night sky to meet the ocean and listen for an invitation to present herself.

Odara was patiently waiting and had fully submitted to the spirit warrior that she was. Her human mind was no longer in control. In this state, it was easy to sit for hours if need be without any motion. Prentice stirred in her lap and then hopped onto the sand. The waves were starting to build, and they were glistening in the early night sky. He looked out at the waves and into the night sky, and then he turned into a bird. With no warning or intention shared, he flew off into the night sky. Odara didn't think twice about it. She knew that whatever he was doing or wherever he was going, was rooted in aiding her.

The sky was quickly getting darker, and the moon had begun to grace the sky. Odara stood up to stretch and admire the difference between the sky at sunset and now. The water that was so bright and full of color before was now a dark rolling force that was moving more quickly and gaining momentum in the sound of the waves.

Odara thought she saw something far off in the water, probably a whale or a dolphin, and she was waiting to see if it would surface again when Prentice reappeared with a few white roses in his claws. He put them at her feet and turned back into himself. Odara picked up the beautiful flowers and smelled them. With her eyes closed, she inhaled their scent and held them up to her nose for a few moments. While she was enjoying the smell of fresh flowers, she heard the faint sound of someone singing. She opened her eyes and saw that the waves were growing taller and coming closer and closer to the shore before breaking. The singing began to get louder, more discernible and seemed to be approaching with the waves.

Odara didn't move – the magnificence of the water was mesmerizing. As a body of waves that any surfer would appreciate began to build and grow, in the near distance the words to a song drifted to her clearly and beautifully: *"Someone needs us on the shore. We'll bring her a way to find out more. Should she be worthy of what she needs, the sea will oblige her, oh yes indeed. But who is this in need of our mother? Not all are worthy, there's been many others. If you are here for the greater good, then meet her you shall and meet her you should."*

Odara and Prentice watched as a huge rolling wave approached the shore. It continued to grow and then broke. When it subsided, there were three women standing at the waters' edge.

The women were long, lean, and beautiful. They were so dark skinned that they wouldn't have been discernible if their skin wasn't glistening in the moonlight, almost as if they had been faintly glittered. They all had long dark locs that were adorned with cowrie and seashells. They were draped in seaweed that elegantly hung on their bodies like formal gowns. In unison, they walked towards Odara, or at least she thought they were walking, but she noticed they weren't leaving individual footprints in the sand. Even though there were three of them, the seaweed train that flowed behind them was the only thing she could see. When they stood face to face, they began to speak. They spoke the same way that they moved, in unison. With big bright eyes and faces that belonged on a magazine cover, they said, "Introduce yourself to our mother and make your needs known. She will hear you through us. Should she acknowledge you, your way to her will be presented. Should she not, what you seek is not here."

Odara looked into the eyes of the three beautiful sea nymphs and spoke. "Mama Yemaya, I am Odara, born Machaneka, created from fire. I am a warrior from the spirit realm for the greater good. I humbly present myself to request your assistance. Because you are the great Mother Protector of children, I am asking to be granted permission to convene with the water that has access to all of the spirits of your daughters. It is my intention to learn from them, so that I can help restore the balance that has been disrupted by the disappearances of those whose destinies were interrupted. With your blessing, Mama Yemaya, I believe that they will reveal to me the information that I need."

The women in front of Odara bowed their heads and locked arms. They began to hum as they rocked back and forth. Prentice circled Odara's feet while watching the women. In one single motion, they raised their heads and outstretched their arms to her. “Your request has been granted. We will provide you with a way the path will reveal itself. You need do nothing until you see our mother rise to greet you.” The incredibly beautiful nymphs turned simultaneously and began moving back towards the waters’ edge. The tide began to roll and increase as they walked into the water. A large wave appeared and rolled towards the shore. When it receded, they were standing on the shoreline next to a boat, and then they turned and walked back into the ocean.

Odara watched them gracefully wading into the semi turbulent ocean water until they disappeared, as if it were a calm lake. She and Prentice walked into the ocean waters to the vessel that had been provided for their journey. It was completely made of conch and abalone shells. Pearls and starfish were sporadically placed to adorn the sides of it. The inside was lined with enormous soft, white pillows for them to sit on. Prentice looked towards the water and said, “The path.” Odara looked out onto the water and saw that the moonlight was shining in a perfect line across the water, headed away from them. “I must transform to assist you here. Use me to get the boat into the ocean, and when we reach our destination, I will change again. Don't forget your offering." Odara got out of the boat and ran back to where they had been sitting to get the bunch of white roses. Then she got into the boat and sat down. Prentice jumped into the boat and turned into a scepter. Odara picked up the scepter and used it to push the boat ahead into the water. The current of the ocean came to life and pulled the boat ahead swiftly.

Odara, watching everything around her on the moonlit path, saw that even though the ocean tide was going in the opposite direction, the boat was moving steadily forward, gliding as if it were being pulled across still waters. She heard Prentices' voice as he changed from the scepter to a small net. "When you see what you need, throw me out to it. I will expand as much as necessary and contain it all. When you pull me in, I will return to this size and resume my original form with everything you need safely stored." Odara placed the net beside her and continued to watch the water for a sign from Yemaya, the ocean mother goddess. Mother of all living things as well as the ocean and the seas. The farther out they traveled, the darker the sky got and the brighter the moon and their path across the ocean seemed to be. Odara was certain a couple of hours had easily passed but even with the hypnotizing sight of the moving waters around her, she was alert and wide eyed. She felt the boat begin to slow down, and she looked around to see if anything was different about her surroundings. When she faced forward again, the boat had come to a complete stop. The ocean waters directly in front of her started to swirl and then right before her eyes, Yemaya rose from the center of swirling waters. Glorious and spectacular, she rose above the water in mermaid form. She was at least eight feet tall with a mane of afro hair that had to be half as big as she was. She wore a crown in her hair made of bright orange coral. Her eyes were kind and she was adorned with pearls and seashells. The colors on the lower half of her body were vibrant blues, greens, purples, and white. The scales seemed to dance as they glittered on her curvaceous lower half. Odara sat up on her knees and held up the roses as an offering to her. Yemaya smiled and waved her hand. The roses flew from Odara's hands to hers and she tucked them into her hair.

"Youuuuu neeeed meeee?" Yemaya's voice was deep and low. She hovered slightly above the water which would raise up in small swirls every few moments and lightly spray her. "I am in search of your daughters whose whereabouts are unknown. There are many of them from one continent that have gone missing in a short period of time. I would like to help them, but I need them to speak to me from a protected space, so I came to you." Odara sat back down and waited for a response. Yemaya rose higher from the water and moved closer to the boat. She spoke again, "Youuuu seeek toooo helppp myyyy childrennn?" Odara looked up at her and replied, "Yes." Yemaya drew back from the boat and submerged under water. She arose swiftly and came to the side of the boat again. Reaching forward with one arm, she opened her hand and said, "Forrr youuu." Odara reached forward and took a small shiny pearl from her hand. Yemaya blew her a kiss and said, "Intoooo the waterrrr. They willllll come. Theyyy willlll alllll come. Helppp myyy childrennnn, Odarrraaa." Yemaya went under water then burst upward into the air. She turned her body and took a dive back into the ocean. She was gone, but she had given Odara permission and a blessing. Odara whispered thank you and looked at the quarter-sized pearl in her hand. She leaned over the side of the boat and dropped the pearl into the water. As soon as it contacted the water, the moonlight that had been the path for the boat began to spread across the water surrounding the boat. It seemed to spread out for miles. The ocean water became almost transparent as small pools began to appear. They grew in number until there were thousands of them, and then they turned into a sea of faces.

Odara stood up in the boat. Scanning for as far as she could see. Female faces of Black women all looking in her direction had covered the surface of the water. She called out to them. "Can you tell me where you are?" Several voices responded with the word no. "Can you tell me who is responsible for you being where you are?" A small voice said, "There are so many of them, they work for something evil. Too many to name." Odara took a deep breath and asked, "Are you still alive?" The waters began to stir, and half of the faces turned completely white, as if they were prepared for a ceremonial burial. Her heart sank. Half of them were no longer alive. She called out again, "Are you being harmed?" Several voices spoke at once, "We are strong in spirit; we believe in our return. Some of us are injured, some of us are used and abused, but we remain hopeful." Odara looked out at the sea of faces. Some of them looked sad, some lost, and some appeared to be crying. She needed to contain the ones whose lives were already lost, so that she could send them to the Sacred Council for final placement or so their spirits could be restored for reincarnation.

Odara knew that what she was going to do next would probably bring whatever evil was behind these disappearances straight to her. Whatever it was will surely be completely pissed off when it realizes that half of what it sought to destroy was gone, and in a place where it couldn't hold their spirits hostage any further. *Bring it on,* she thought, *it will be my pleasure to destroy you.* She threw the net that Prentice had assumed the form of into the water and watched it begin to expand.

While the net was expanding, she spread out her arms and called out to the Sacred Council; "I call for the collective powers of the Sacred Council to block, protect, and guide the spirits of these thousands of women whose lives were shortened by the evils of mankind. I bind all of them as one unit to be transferred to the realm of the heavens where they will be restored and nurtured until the time comes for them to assume another life and finish what they were destined to do. Those who have not another life to live, deserve to rest in peace. I send them to you for a graceful resting place. I do this now with no lapse in time." She pulled the net out of the water and it instantly shrank back to the small net that it was originally. Holding it in her hands she said, "Release the deceased to me, Prentice."

Prentice turned back into himself for a few seconds and dropped a small clear stone from his mouth. Odara picked it up and held it in her palm. She felt the temperature in her hand begin to increase at once. The stone, in reaction to the temperature of her palm nearing that of fire itself, doubled in size and began to cloud. Odara held her palm up to the sky as the stone began to crack and small beams of light started breaking through the cracks. In the next few moments, the night sky was filled with thousands of tiny streams of light shooting upward from her palm. The fire from her hand was propelling them forward. She heard the sound of wings in motion, lots of them, and she heard Prentice say, "Spectacular!"

At first, she couldn't see what it was that he saw because the lights were plentiful and so bright. She adjusted her focus and saw hundreds of large eagles swooping and swirling, creating a barrier around the light streams as they ascended. *Isis*. She knew that it was Isis who'd sent a sentry of eagles to ensure that nothing interfered with the ascension process. As the last stream of light shot out of the stone in her hand, the stone turned completely black, and a small covering of gold enveloped it. The stone was literally smoldering in her hand and she looked up to see that the eagles had aligned themselves into a formation in the sky that looked like one giant set of wings. "Thank you, Isis!" she yelled into the sky, and the wings flapped and were gone.

Odara sat down on one of the pillows in the boat and looked about. The path that had led them to the spot they were in had illuminated again for their return to land. She looked at Prentice and he seemed to have grown some in size. She didn't question it. She told him, "We will return to land and stay in the city overnight. I am famished and my spirit says that tomorrow morning is when we move. Tomorrow, Prentice, we will be at war."

A warrior's strongest weapon

is their heart

9
Odara's Defense

Odara looked out across the Pacific Ocean at the gently moving water. The light that illuminated the path across the water back to shore, radiated against the dark blueish green and sparkled. She was about to command transport when the three sea nymphs that greeted her on the shore appeared at the helm of the boat. They rose out of a swirl of water and then descended beneath them again. Once they were out of sight, the boat began to move swiftly across the illuminated path towards the shore.

Odara sat back with Prentice in her lap and thought about the Augustin women. She would have to get back to them before engaging in battle because they needed to be protected. She couldn't risk anything going after them while she was engaged in warfare. The memory of Intisar with tears streaming down her face was embedded in her mind. The tapestries with holes growing and spreading was almost haunting her. Odara hoped that with the placement of half of the missing women in a final place of peaceful rest, some of the holes were gone or had mended.

As Odara was thinking about the Augustin women, back at the Augustin Home, the twins Linda and Ola, were simultaneously discussing her. After the discussion held the previous morning during teatime, Linda and Ola went back to the workshop and started to survey their work from the past month. They too had noticed some small things but had dismissed them as oversights. This day, however, they decided to take a look and talk about what they were noticing. "Intisar and Zora's realms have direct impact on one another. We're in a completely different part of the universe. Do you think it's possible that there is a universal ripple effect?"

Linda sat quietly, waiting for her twin Ola to answer her. Ola was intensely surveying the stories of her tapestry, trying to make sense of it all. She didn't answer her twin's question. She responded with, "What do you make of Odara?" We know that her presence was requested through prayer. We know that on the day she was supposed to speak with all of us, she only talked to Intisar and then she was gone. What is her purpose in all of this? I felt very *safe* for lack of a better word, when she arrived. Where is she from? What does she do? Should we tell her when she returns what we see in our tapestries?

I have a ton of questions because I don't like the way this feels, these areas where my loom seemed to literally jump and skip spaces. What do you think?" Linda was staring at her loom. She was just as puzzled about what Odara's presence in their household was about as her twin was. She looked at her paternal twin. Linda was grateful that they shared the same workspace and that they could usually have conversations without words. True to the testament of most twins, they could *feel* one another. The realms that they were assigned to had planetary life that had nothing to do with Earth at all, and the life forces in that realm were significantly more advanced than the human beings that Intisar was recording. Without trying to go any further, Linda and Ola sat down at their looms and went back to work.

Odara's concentration went back to where she was and what had transpired throughout the night. The boat was moving rapidly, and Odara was able to make out the outline of the shore. Prentice sat up in her lap, and they watched as the nymphs would take to the air from the water from time to time. They looked like dolphins or mermaids at play when they emerged and flipped through the air then submerged again. Shortly after seeing the shoreline, they approached it. When the boat was safely on the beach, Odara and Prentice stepped back onto land. The sea nymphs stood at the edge of the water and then turned and re-entered the ocean.

The boat followed them. As they were swimming away, Odara heard them singing again. *"Odara's plight is a mighty one, she will not rest until she's done. We know she hears our sisters' screams; she knows they all had hopes and dreams, Odara is the living key to help restore the harmony. We know she'll fight and hopes she wins, for this is a battle that needs to end."*

As their voices drifted farther away, Odara stood in the sand with Prentice next to her and stared in the direction in which they swam. She raised her arms and sent a message through the wind of the night. "White roses for the sea, please!" Within moments, a breeze swooped in and thousands of white roses dropped onto the water. As far as Odara could see, a blanket of roses covered the ocean and the smell of fresh flowers permeated the air. She knelt and with outstretched arms said, "For you, Mama Yemaya. Thank you." She rose to her feet and picked Prentice up into her arms. Before she could turn away to transport them to the inner city, an enormous wave rose, heading towards them and the shore. Sitting atop of that wave was the mighty Yemaya. She stood up on the wave like a skilled surfer and held her arms out. With a downward sweeping gesture, Yemaya skimmed her hands across the top of the wave then stood back up. She scooped up about twenty-five roses. She raised her hands above her head and let them fall. They ended up all over her beautiful mane of hair. Yemaya blew a kiss to Odara, and in an instant, she disappeared in the wave. The wave crashed the shore, and when the water rolled back towards the ocean, something was lying in the sand. Odara walked to the edge of the water and picked it up. She had been gifted a gold cuff that had a stunning seashell in the center of it. She held it up to her ear. "Whennnn youuu neeeeed meee IIIII ammmm heeerrreee." Yemaya's voice came through the seashell clear and strong. Odara put the cuff on her wrist and admired the beauty of it. Still holding Prentice, she drew a large circle in the sand with her foot. Once it was drawn, Odara stepped into the middle of the circle. "A full night of the finest comfort for rest and a full day of recovery for preparation. Take me there now."

Odara held Prentice tightly as the wind and orbs of light surrounded them. When the wind settled and she could see clearly, she was standing in the window of a hotel room overlooking the city of San Francisco, California. She set Prentice down and he began to stretch and walk around the room. The view of San Francisco was breathtaking. Fully lit up with the night lights of the city. The skyline and view of the ocean from afar had a calming effect on her. Odara took a deep breath and drew the curtains. Taking a look around the hotel room, she saw the "Marquis Marriott" notepad by the telephone. *Nice*, she thought to herself. They were in the one-bedroom presidential suite with the Bay view. The room design was modern, spacious, and extremely comfortable. Prentice had curled up on the sofa and was peacefully resting. Odara opened the closet and took the courtesy soft plush robe and slippers out. Sitting on the king-sized bed that felt like a piece of heaven, she undressed and went into the bathroom. She ran a hot bath in the oversized tub and was glad to see that it had a whirlpool. After pouring the complimentary lavender scented bath gel into the water to provide some bubbles, Odara stepped into the tub and sat down as the tub filled up. She turned the water off, turned on the whirlpool, and laid back with her eyes closed to let her body fully relax.

The last couple of days had taken a toll on Odara's physical body. The water pressure from the whirlpool was exhilarating. She felt the tension in her back and legs slowly begin to release and dissipate. While laying back in the tub, her mind began to wander. Her mind went to her last assignment before she was promoted.

The entity that she had to battle to protect Sudan's family was an angry, vicious spirit that was bent on revenge. What she was dealing with now was something so much bigger, something more sinister and uglier. Odara smiled at the thought of her new Chateau in the South of France. The beauty and splendor of it all. Her thoughts shifted to the Baobab tree in Senegal, meeting Kelly and Apollo, and what she saw on the walls inside of the hill. All of that combined with her trip to the Pacific Ocean and summoning Yemaya was playing over and over again in her mind. Every piece led to another one but no full resolve. Reflecting on the Augustin women and their responsibility to capture the lives of all living beings, in every dimension and on every plane in the universe, in the weaving of tapestries, was mind-blowing. Now here she was in the year 2019, and there were 64,000 African American women missing. Gone without a trace, some of them had already been gone for years.

Physically she felt like someone had removed a body part from her. Odara understood that a balance must be restored. The most critical part of this assignment was the balance that had been disrupted. If the disappearances continued, the tapestries that Intisar was assigned to for planet

Earth would continue to unravel and fall apart. If that happened, there would be a ripple effect of lives falling apart. That would lead to dismay, hopelessness, and many open portals for the enemies of the greater good of the earth to divide and multiply. The latter option was a non-option. She had to get to whatever was causing the disappearances, and she had to put an end to it.

She had already been warned that this battle was to be fought in spirit and flesh. She wasn't afraid, just anxious to put a stop to the madness. Odara constantly dozed off in the lavender scented bubbly water. She took her time luxuriating and then bathed her body. When she stepped out of the tub, she dried off and put on the robe and slippers. It felt like she had been wrapped in a giant teddy bear hug. She walked back into the bedroom of the suite and got into the bed. Prentice jumped down from the sofa and jumped onto the bed. He was extremely quiet, almost seemingly contemplative. He looked at Odara with a smile in his eyes and then he curled up on one of the pillows on the bed. It was only a matter of moments before they both were sound asleep. While asleep, Odara began dreaming. She saw the Augustin women at their looms, tirelessly weaving their tapestries. She saw all of them clearly, but this time, when she saw the twin matriarchs on their knees praying, they weren't crying or in distress. They were peaceful and still. Noting that this had to be a good sign, she looked around for Intisar. Intisar was at her loom, she was weaving, and not only was she weaving, she had a slight smile on her face.

Then she turned and looked directly at Odara. The hurt, anguished look from their last encounter was gone. Odara told her, "It's not over yet." Intisar turned back to her loom and said, "I know, I'm just glad that you're here." Odara turned over in her sleep and the dream ended there. She opened her eyes, smiled, and drifted back to sleep.

Success is what happens

when preparation meets opportunity

10
Before the Storm

The sunlight that was able to creep past the closed curtains in the hotel suite was just enough to wake Odara. She stretched out and turned over. Prentice was already awake, and he was sitting on the edge of the bed bathing himself. Odara didn't want to move. The stillness and peace of the suite was wonderful, and the bed she was lying in was comfortable. It provided the best sleep she'd had in a long time away from home. She sat up and asked Prentice if he wanted to join her for breakfast. "Breakfast?" he responded. "It's almost 1 p.m. Perhaps you mean a late lunch?" Odara looked at the clock on the nightstand adjacent to the bed and saw that it was indeed afternoon time. She was completely relaxed and felt rested. She got out of bed and went into the restroom to clean herself up and get dressed. Prentice came to the bathroom door and spoke to her. "I have very old friends who reside in the city. A suggestion for dining this afternoon was provided early this morning when I went out for a walk." Odara answered through the door, "How did you go out for a walk? Never mind.

I'm forgetting who you are. I hope your friends suggested somewhere I can get something soulful *and* healthy. I'm not in the mood for basic American fare." Odara opened the door and looked down at Prentice. She could swear that he was almost twice the size that he was when he first appeared on the road at the Augustin house. Prentice looked up at her and before answering, took the form of a casually dressed gentleman. "In answer to your thoughts, yes, I have grown in size since we first met. As my capabilities expand and your assignment grows in depth, my physical form will show growth from time to time. I won't get too much bigger physically, but my core is reacting to your needs and expanding inside. In answer to your question about the restaurant suggested for a meal, it is both soulful and healthy. You will be able to get the flavors you may be craving along with the satisfaction of it not being unhealthy. It's a new spot called "Voodoo Love," only a few minutes from here on Howard Street. My friends tell me that it is contemporary Louisiana food. Shall we try it?"

Prentice, in the form of a man was quite attractive. Caramel skin, broad shoulders, and clean cut. Dressed in a pair of jeans and a black sweater, Odara was wondering if his original form was that of a cat or if he was assigned to be a cat for this assignment with her. Remembering that he could read her mind, she cut her thoughts off. “Yes, let’s go there. I need some good food and anything southern or Creole sounds perfect.” She was putting on her shoes as she answered him. When she looked up at his 6-foot 2-inch frame, he was staring at her smiling. “One day we will have that conversation. I am many things, Odara, and proud to have always been on the right side of them.”

They decided to walk to the restaurant. By foot it was about a twenty-minute walk. The air was fresh and brisk but not too cold. They walked and chatted about the sights of the city. Odara told Prentice that the last time she was in California, it was open territory. Their twenty-minute walk passed quickly. They looked up and saw that they were in front of the restaurant. The smell of deliciousness coming from inside affirmed that they had made the right choice.

Odara and Prentice, probably appearing as a young couple to outsiders, entered the restaurant. A pretty young woman greeted them, and they were seated at a table. Odara looked at the menu and got excited. She couldn’t help it. Good food would always be her personal delight when she was in a physical body. There was a physical menu and the menu was written on the walls in chalk. The atmosphere was cozy and warm. It wasn't overcrowded or congested, and they had arrived just after the lunch rush. Odara liked the place. When the waitress returned to take their orders, Prentice had decided on the Cajun salmon plate. Odara ordered the shrimp and grits with a side of collard greens and cornbread. Initially, she was going to have a full vegan meal, but the shrimp and grits was calling her. She really wanted a glass of wine—or two, but she never drank anything before entering spiritual warfare, and that was where she was headed, possibly in the next few hours. Prentice held up his glass of water and made a toast to progress and victory. She toasted with him and looked around the restaurant. Jazz music played in the background and enhanced her mood. A woman sitting alone a few tables away caught her attention. Prentice was chattering about his friend's impression of the restaurant but her attention was on the woman who was looking back at her like she had something to say.

Prentice felt the energy and stopped his conversation. The waitress delivered their food to the table and Odara's attention went to her meal. Prentice was now looking at the young woman who was reading a book while enjoying her meal. Every now and again, she would look back at him. He smiled at Odara and said, "A friend is here." Odara looked over at the young woman again, she nodded a greeting towards her and then started eating her food.

The first bite was heavenly. Odara was impressed. Everything on her plate was perfectly cooked. She had finished her shrimp and grits and was starting on her cornbread and collard greens when she remembered she wasn't dining alone. She glanced at Prentice and he was looking at her totally amused. "I guess you really needed that. I don't believe you were breathing while you attacked those shrimp and grits."

Odara laughed out loud and then apologized. "I almost forgot you were sitting there. I'm sorry, how's your Cajun salmon?" Prentice smiled and said, "No problem, enjoy your food. My salmon is perfectly cooked and seasoned. I didn't expect for the portions to be so ample." They both laughed and continued to eat. The waitress checked on them a couple of times with a smile and an extremely pleasant disposition. They finished eating and paid the bill, leaving a hearty tip for great service. Odara and Prentice stood up and prepared to leave. As they were walking out of the door, the young woman who had been watching them rose to leave as well.

While waiting across the street, Odara was about to tell Prentice what needed to be done and what she was about to do when the young woman approached them. "Excuse me, this might sound weird, but I need to share something with you." Prentice honed in on her presence and surveyed her from head to toe.

After a moment, his eyes relaxed and Odara answered her. "What can we do for you?" The young woman introduced herself; "My name is Jahiya Celestial Love. I wasn't trying to be rude by staring while you were eating. It's just that when I saw you come into the restaurant, Ihad a strong feeling that I was supposed to meet you. I believe I have something that is meant for you."

Jahiya reached into her purse and pulled out an amulet that was on a fine gold chain. "This has been in my family for at least twenty generations. Every time it is passed down, the person who receives it is told that it should stay in the family until whomever is in possession of it meets someone that they think it should go to.

My ancestors were from the Mayan culture. The story is, this amulet was made by priests and blessed for purification and protection. When I saw you, a voice in my head told me to give it to you. I don't know why, or who you are, but I know that I'm supposed to. I hope that it helps with whatever it is that you're about to do."

Odara was at a loss for words. Jahiya handed the amulet to Odara. Odara took the amulet from her and instantly felt a light flood through her. Jahiya and Prentice both took a step back from

Odara. "Wow!" Jahiya exclaimed, "I knew I was right! I knew it!" Odara, puzzled, looked at Prentice. "A veil of light just covered you, like an Angel just hovered over you." He was obviously caught off guard by the amulet's show of power as well. Odara put the amulet around her neck and extended her hands to Jahiya.

Jahiya was still in amazement when Odara started speaking to her. Holding Jahiya's hands, Odara said, "Nothing is by coincidence. You have been obedient, gracious, and selfless by giving me this amulet. I am going to give you something in return. You will feel your hands warm up but don't be alarmed, it's just a transfer from my spirit to yours. Precious young, Jahiya, if you are ever in danger or great trouble, all you need say is, 'Odara please help.' I will either appear myself, or I will send you the help that you need, and you will know that it is me who sent you assistance. I speak this to be so from this moment for the rest of your natural life."

Odara and Jahiya held hands until the temperature of her palms began to decrease. She released Jahiya's hands and said, "Be well, young Queen, and thank you." Jahiya smiled and then wrapped her arms around Odara. Odara accepted the embrace and kissed her on her forehead. Prentice spoke up, "We need to head out." Jahiya said, "Thank you. Thank you so much. I don't know exactly what just happened, but I know it was awesome. I feel amazing!"

Then with a smile, she turned and started walking away. As Jahiya walked away slowly, she started humming. Odara told Prentice, "Let's let her see." Prentice said, "Why not? I like her." They stood on the corner for another moment and waited. As expected, Jahiya looked back and waved goodbye once more. While she was waving, Odara commanded the wind for travel, "Ascend, third realm, second dimension, to the Augustin house!" Jahiya stopped in her tracks and watched with wide eyes as the wind and a swirl of light encircled Odara and Prentice, lifted them into the sky, and they were gone. "No one is going to believe this. Not one single person.

Wow." Jahiya spoke to herself out loud and continued walking with a smile on her face and in her heart.

11
Odara's Attack

Odara and Prentice arrived at the front door of the Augustin house. Prentice had reassumed his form of a black Persian cat and was standing next to Odara, waiting for her to knock so they could go inside. The night was still and warm. As usual, before Odara could knock at the door, Lisa opened the door and greeted them. "Glad to see you've returned safely, Ms. Odara and Prentice. Everything in your room has been freshly prepared for you. If you're hungry, there is food in the kitchen that I can warm for you." Odara thanked her and declined the offer for food. They entered the house and went directly into their room.

Once inside of the bedroom, Odara pulled out the satchel that held all the things that she had been gifted for defense for her assignment. She told Prentice, "I'm going to have to disrupt the flow of the house to protect the Augustin women. I'll need to have them all present at once. I'm also going to have to absorb everything that I've been gifted into my body.

Once the weavers and this house is protected, we will immediately go into warfare. My goal is to find out where the remaining women who are alive and missing are located and have them returned to their families. I'm troubled in my spirit by the lack of concern about their absences. Why wasn't there an all-out outrage or some sort of organized effort to recover them. I sensed almost nothing of a unified front while we were in the United States. Even more disturbing to me was that there was a chaotic disorder to the energy there. The tapestries are being affected by those women, but there are so many other horrific things happening. Missing children, human trafficking, organ stealing…I felt it all. It was almost endless. For now, though, I will focus on what is present in this assignment. It is most definitely troubling what's happening in 2019 in the United States. Definitely troubling indeed." Prentice looked at Odara and sent his response to her mind. "I have seen the horrors of man's actions for thousands of years. Nothing surprises nor frightens me. You can make a difference here. I am here to ensure that you are successful in this assignment. The battle that we are stepping into will bring out the best of the warrior in you. You will be in awe of yourself. I am ready and so are you. Whatever is behind this is much bigger than any one man's sick desires or actions. We will find out what it is, and we will do what needs to be done."

Odara took a deep breath and looked over the contents of her satchel: the angel feathers that Jerod had left for her; the Brugmansia, "Angels Trumpets" in powdered form; and the salve from Amaterasu. She took them all and placed them in the windowsill. The moon was full and bright. It shone on the items as she placed her hands over them and said, "Become one." One at a time, the items on the windowsill began to dissipate. As each one was absorbed through her palms, Odara was jolted by a quickening in her body. Her arms rippled and she felt her blood pumping and coursing throughout her entire being. When there was nothing left to absorb, she thanked the moon for its divine light. Odara was ready. She turned to Prentice and said, "Time to protect the women of this house."

Odara and Prentice walked down the hallway towards the drawing room of the Augustin home. She wasn't sure what type of reaction she would get from the sisters for stopping them from doing what they did every day, all day and night. She glanced at the walls in the long hallway. There were no pictures on them. In the places where she had once seen incredible paintings were mirrors. Several of them in different shapes and sizes. She caught a glimpse of herself and stopped walking. Prentice halted when she stopped. She hadn't seen herself in a mirror in quite a while and what she saw was not what she'd seen the last time that she looked in one.

Her hair, a free-flowing mane of an afro, was ornately decorated with cowrie shells threaded in a design around her forehead and temple, framing her face. Along with that, she had a few streaks of silver hair mixed into her curls. Her skin and eyes were bright and glowing. The muscles in her arms and legs were strong and well defined. She was wearing, unbeknownst to her, a fitted one-piece black bodysuit that had the Adinkra symbols for justice, hope, truth, strength, and vigilance, in white across the top of the bodice. Hanging from her ears were large gold discs. Around her neck was the amulet that Jahiya had given her, and on one wrist was the cuff gifted to her by Yemaya. On the other wrist was a gold cuff that had a disc in the same shape as the ones on her ears. She had on black thigh high flat boots that were laced with gold from the ankle to the top of the thigh. Realizing that she had been prepared for war, she took in the visual of herself and was proud. She looked fearless and strong. Prentice looked up at her and said, "You look like a badass." Odara smiled at him and said, "We're about to see how deep that goes, Prentice. Tonight."

Odara and Prentice walked into the drawing room, the largest room in the Augustin home.

Odara was surprised to see that all the sisters and their mother Bessie, along with her twin Ethel B, had gathered and were seated. They seemed to have been waiting for her. Once again, they were a spectacular sight. This time though, they weren't wearing an array of brightly colored formal wear as they had for Sunday dinner. The Augustin women were in all white dresses. Every single one of them. Mama Bessie stood up and spoke; "We were told to gather here and wait for you. We were also told to do everything that you say to do, as you say to do it. It came to me during prayer this morning. We understand that our home may possibly be in some sort of danger." Odara looked at every one of them before she spoke. She saw in their eyes that they were not afraid. They were a strong group and the strength and energy in the room was powerful. "I believe that it is possible that I may be engaging something close to pure evil.

Because of that, anything is possible in the form of distraction and or retaliation. I cannot be sure of any type of attack against you, but I will not risk you being unprotected. Please follow me outside." After Odara spoke, she started walking to the front door. The Augustin women and Prentice followed her into the front yard. She told Lisa to close the front door, light all the candles in the house, and have the kitchen staff join her at the dining room table. They were not to move until the family re-entered the home.

Lisa closed the front door and set about following Odara's instructions. Odara started with Mama Bessie in front of the house, about fifty feet from the front door. "Stand here, please Mother. Everyone else follow me." Mama Bessie stood where she had been told to and the others followed Odara. Odara spread the daughters and Aunt Ethel B out around the perimeter of the house until they had formed a circle around it, with each of them instructed to wait for her instructions. When the circle was complete, she asked Prentice for assistance. "I need a circle to surround the women, about twenty feet away from them so I can create a barrier." Prentice nodded at Odara and walked over to where Mama Bessie stood. He turned and walked twenty feet away from her and then stopped. Prentice scratched at the ground and drew a line in the soft dirt with his paw. Next, he walked to where each sister was standing and repeated the process. He stood twenty feet away, pawing out a line in the earth. When he was back in the front of the house, he walked to where he had drawn the first line. Prentice dug at the area where he had begun until the line was gouged into the ground. With a small pile of dirt in front of him, he dropped down onto his belly and blew the dirt into the air. When he did so, each line that he had drawn adjacent to all of the women began to expand in length until they had all connected to form a complete circle around them.

When Odara saw that the women had been encompassed by an outer barrier in the ground, she went to them one by one and told them to spread their arms out from the sides of their bodies with their palms facing away from them. After they were all in that position, she walked to all of them and released a small orb of fire that hovered in the air between each set of outstretched hands. Once that was done, Odara walked to the front of the house where Prentice had initiated the protective barrier. Odara stuck her hand partially into the open ground where Prentice had created a small opening by digging the earth out. "Surround and then connect above this home and these women, protect but do not burn them. Let them be untouchable." Odara made her command, and a small flame began to follow and spread throughout the circle surrounding the Augustin family. When the flame reached where it had begun, it shot up into a wall of fire, growing in height until it was higher than the house; you couldn't see what was behind the wall of flames. Prentice stepped back and watched as Odara walked through the wall of flames and disappeared. Once inside of the flame barrier, Odara went to where Intisar, the oldest of the Augustin daughters stood. There was an orb between Intisar and her mother Mama Bessie on one side of her, and another orb between Intisar and her sister Glenda on the other side of her. Odara held her hands out in the direction of each orb and commanded, "Connect!" The orb expanded into a thread of fire connecting Intisar to her mother and her sister. Odara went between Glenda and Ola, Ola and Linda, Linda and Zora, Zora and Samara, Samara and Aunt Ethel B, and lastly, Aunt Ethel B and Mama Bessie, until they were all connected by the threads of fire between their outstretched palms. Odara felt a power that she had never felt before. Using the fire that she was created from made her feel more alive. She felt like she was getting stronger being surrounded by it. Without further thought, she took to the air, and once over the top of the house, she spread her arms out and brought her hands together over her head. With a loud clap, she commanded, "Connect!" The wall of fire that surrounded the Augustin home now stretched high and created a full dome over the house. Odara, still airborne over the house, spoke aloud, "I call on all of the protective forces in the universe for a seal over and around this home and the land that it rests on until I bid it to be released. Let it be impenetrable until my voice seeks your assistance again."

Odara returned to the ground and watched as her request was granted. The magnolia trees in the yard began to multiply until they were as dense as a forest. As they multiplied, they quadrupled in size and their branches began to grow and intertwine. It was only a matter of minutes before the entire estate was a thick fortress of a wall of connected trees. It was so full that you could no longer see the dome of fire that covered the house. After the trees had weaved a full barrier. A shower of light came from the sky and covered the entire property. It touched every inch and then took the form of a large box of light, completely sealing the Augustin property.

Odara stood where the road met the walkway to the Augustin home. The entire property and the Augustin women were now enshrouded with protection. As she was looking at the encapsulated property that was no longer visible nor recognizable, she heard great wings flapping. She thought Jerod was approaching and braced herself to lay eyes on him. It wasn't Jerod. A large winged animal was slowly approaching the perimeter where she and Prentice stood. A massive Sphinx landed right in front of them. Prentice dropped down and lowered his head. The Sphinx lowered its head to Odara and Prentice then took back into the air. They watched as it flew higher and higher until it was directly over the center of the protective light barrier that covered the property. The Sphinx landed atop the barrier, assumed a position to sit, and with its head facing forward, rested on top of the covering. Odara was absolutely certain that nothing would be able to attack the women or their home and survive it.

Odara walked to the center of the road and was about to summon a portal to the dark realm when the ground began shake. A loud rumbling ensued, and her palms went instantaneously to fiery hot. Prentice reared back and then increased in size until he was almost eight feet tall. A large billow of dust and dirt surrounded them and when it cleared, nearly one hundred men and women, of several different nationalities were in its place. Odara scanned them as they stood glaring viciously at her and Prentice. They were all human, and they were all in a rage. They had been sent by whatever was controlling them to stop her from entering the portal to the dark realm. That meant that she was a threat to the discord, a strong one, and that gave her more hope – but something wasn't right. Even though they were human beings, obviously normal human beings from planet Earth, there was an undercurrent of strength and power that was not earthly. No one moved. She stared at them and they stared at her. Then she got it. They were all being controlled and had been inhabited by something dark and sinister. Their biggest weakness was that they were unaware that they had been inhabited, and some of them may not have been evil at their core. Odara knew what she had to do, and it had to be concise and quick.

Suddenly, the crowd of enraged men and women tried to converge on her and Prentice. Prentice pounced, and with a single swipe of his paw, cat claws flew outward, piercing at least twenty of them like finely sharpened swords. Several men and women in the group who were closest to Odara, physically jumped onto her, pummeling her with fists and kicking her savagely. Odara curled herself into a ball and then opened up with her palms facing the sky, releasing an enormous cloud of Brugsmansia into the atmosphere. Her attackers were instantly affected by the intensity of the cloud burst. The Brugsmansia was extremely potent and was inhaled by all of the people who surrounded her. They began to lose connection with reality and became disoriented. Some of the stronger ones were still trying to attack but Prentice sent another wave of cat claws flying, and they were struck to the ground in extreme pain. In the next moment, some of them began to hallucinate and fight out against the air. Prentice lowered himself, and Odara climbed onto his back. When he stood up straight, Odara locked her legs into his collar and said, "Spin, Prentice!" Prentice started to spin in a circle. As he spun around, Odara opened her arms and released a flurry of Angel feathers into the air. Prentice instinctively knew to stop when everything went silent. Odara looked about at the mob that had been sent to attack her. They were all drug induced by the Brugsmansia and now immobilized by the Angel feathers that had touched each and every one of them. She quickly did a self-check for injuries from the attack and found that she had none.

Prentice circled her twice and then turned into a large jeweled dagger. "Use me to open the portal to the dark realm" was the message he sent to Odara. She picked up the dagger and drove it into the ground with one deep strike. "Reveal yourself, doorway to darkness!" The ground parted where she had struck it and a doorway appeared. It was dark and misty, and it sent a chill down Odara's spine. Prentice regained his form and told Odara to brace herself. She grounded herself as Prentice walked back several feet from her. With a running start, Prentice ran towards her *and then jumped into her!* Odara's body spread eagled upon the impact. An intense scream came from the center of her spirit as Prentice became one with her. She felt his strength and capabilities become a part of her and her body began to levitate above the ground. Every muscle in her body rippled, her afro blew in the wind and turned completely silver, and everything around her that could be seen was magnified. Odara immediately hurled herself into the portal.

Odara landed in the dark realm and immediately felt the heaviness of the darkness. She looked around and saw dark silhouettes of trees, animals, and what appeared to be people. Nothing was clearly discernable, just dark moving shadows and an indescribable feeling of ugliness. She knew that what she had come for would come to her. She was an intruder, a warrior for the good things, and this place and everything in it would be unwelcoming. She focused in on her surroundings. She could hear whispers, hissing sounds, and saw different forms scurrying about quickly. Something was beginning to take form a few feet away from her. Prepared for battle, she gave its manifestation her full attention.

A dark glob of strange matter was rising from the ground. It was bulbous and slowly forming into something similar to human in shape. As it formed, the hissing sounds around Odara got louder. She noticed that the shadows and moving forms she'd seen were retreating. The form was growing taller. It looked like something was trying to break through a blob of some sort of liquid. It stopped growing in height and Odara saw slits in what would've been a face of a normal being. The slits opened and yellowish eyes peered at her. The being had assimilated a somewhat disfigured human shape that was encompassed by a moving liquid. The being stared at her with hatred in its yellow eyes. She knew that it was not pleased at all to be in her presence.

"You have caused much dissention. I underestimated you. My newest sentry failed to prevent your entrance through the portal. Why are you here? You are not welcome here, and if I can help it, you will not leave. I will answer your questions, and then I will destroy you. You will be my greatest acquisition. Now, what do you want?" The voice coming from the entity was male, old, low, gravely, and labored. It sounded like it had to put forth considerable effort to speak. While it was speaking, it made no effort to move towards Odara, but the liquid substance that it was encased in was constantly moving. It looked like crude oil traveling from head to toe and then back again.

Odara spoke to the being with force and definition. "I have come to find the missing African American women from the United States. I will leave here knowing where they are, and I will return them to their families. As you know, the women whose lives were lost have already been sent to a place of safe, peaceful rest. They will all be returned to Earth in another body and given the opportunity to fulfill their destinies. You do not have the right to possess innocent people, fill them with your filth, and use them to commit horrific actions. You do not have the right to disrupt the lives of innocent people and cause them harm. You will not destroy me, and I will leave with what I came here for. Your sentry was disabled, and I will destroy all of them if necessary."

The being made a strange sound that it repeated, and then it started to laugh. The laughter continued and turned into a howl. "The women you speak of, they are here." It put its arms across its chest area and then opened them. The faces of the missing women began to flash across the opening that the being revealed. The sight of them made Odara's stomach drop. She gasped as the faces continued to flash one by one. Some of them were in tears, some were obviously in a panic, some were staring blankly, and some were screaming for help. The being covered its chest and laughed aloud again. Odara could still hear the women, begging and pleading to go home. "They will go nowhere with you, and the women who weave those tapestries will join them. They are under attack as we speak. I am not concerned for the sentry that you disabled, for we are many. I even have children that do what I say. You lose today, Odara of the second sentry for the Sacred Council." The entity laughed again after it spoke and then started to move slowly towards her.

Odara spoke with force again, "I will give you one opportunity to live. Where are the women I seek?"

The being didn't answer her. It stopped its slow approach towards her, and at once, moved with lightning speed. Odara was caught off guard by the speed and aggression. Before she knew it, the entity had its hands around her neck, and she was lifted into the air off of her feet. It was incredibly strong. She was being strangled. She knew that her body would not survive being choked so forcefully. She opened her palms and sent massive fire into the being. It shrieked but did not lose force in its grip around her throat.

The being laughed aloud, "Your body is no good here, Odara. As you lose life, I will absorb all that you know and are. There is nothing that comes here that I cannot and will not destroy.

Die now, Odara. Die now!" Odara was heading towards losing consciousness and she heard the voice of Prentice in her head. "Liquefy and infuse him. He will not attack himself."

When Prentice jumped into Odara's body, she acquired the ability to shapeshift and still execute her own powers. She looked the being in its eyes and released herself. To the surprise of her assailant, Odara's body dissolved into a liquid and began to cover its body and merge with the fluid that covered it. Odara spread herself out onto the entity and felt herself merging with the form she was covering. It was an ugly feeling. She could still hear the voices of the women somewhere inside of the entity. It was writhing and struggling as she merged with it. The light from her goodness was penetrating and blending throughout its body and it didn't know how to defend itself. "Inside," she heard Prentice say. She focused on matching the consistency of the blob so that she could blend better into it. Odara heard a woman say, "This way," and she followed the voice deeper into the entity. Just as she reached a nucleus where the voices were coming from, the entity screeched, "Noooo!" Odara felt a strange sensation and tried to go into the nucleus. She realized that the form was changing and felt pressure surrounding her. It was starting to solidify. She was sure that she didn't have time to go into the nucleus and extract the whereabouts of the women before the being had completely solidified. If it was successful, she would be trapped inside of this spirit monster. If she solidified and removed herself, her physical body would be in great danger. Odara decided that if she wouldn't leave this place with what she came for, at least she could put an end to this particular evil.

Odara, still liquefied, pulled herself into one space inside of the entity and formed a sphere. She channeled all of the fire inside of her and began an incantation. "I call on the great Isis to help me disburse whatever is necessary to destroy this evil. I speak death into this being, with no re-emergence. There will be one less force of darkness attacking the lives of African American women. Sohellata, Nasphella, Kamatulla!"

Odara felt the body strengthening and solidifying, but it was too late. As soon as she finished the incantation, she imploded the being. Fire and screams filled the air. She had regained her form and instinctively produced an orb to encase herself. She watched as the fire she used to implode the being turned bright blue and then white. Isis had answered her call. In the next moment, it was completely gone. The screaming and shrieking had stopped and there was now silence. Odara was devastated. Now there was no way to find the remaining women. With angry tears flowing down her face, she called out to them, "I will not stop looking for you. I will command a nation to seek you out, you are not forgotten!" Her voice echoed throughout the vast dark land that she stood on. She knelt and struck the ground with her fist, sending a wall of fire up. Odara stood up and commanded the portal, "To the Augustin house!"

Peace be Still

12
Closure

Odara exited the portal in the exact spot that she had entered into the dark realm. The people who had been sent to stop her from entering the portal were still spread out on the road in front of the Augustin home. Hours had passed and they were still disoriented from inhaling the Brugsmansia. Some of them were looking around confused. Odara looked at the ones who had been injured from being pierced by Prentices' claws. They seemed to have no idea where they were or why they were there. There were a few still babbling. Odara waited a moment before speaking. She thought that Prentice would be exiting her body by now. Obviously, she still needed him to assist her from inside even though the danger was over. She raised her hand and spoke to all of them.

"You don't know where you are or why, and it doesn't matter. You were under the influence of something evil that used you to kidnap, steal, and kill innocent people for quite some time. For some of you, it has been years. Your crimes, although atrocious, were not committed by you while in complete control of your faculties, and that is the only reason that you will leave here alive. I wish you had some memory of what you've done. It would be helpful to me. I know that you do not because the entity that I just destroyed took all memory of your actions with it in its demise. I am going to release you from immobility and send you to your homes and families. I bind you with a covering that will not allow you to be used again for anything other than good. You will not remember any of this.

When you return to your homes, it will be the same time and day that it was when you were taken possession of. You will have the opportunity to reclaim the time that you were used for evil and do right by it." Odara raised her hands and said, "Release and return!" The Angel feathers that had covered the mob took to the air and bound themselves together, then the bundle flew into her hands. "To the United States, free of memory and charged with protection for the rest of your lives, Ascend!" Odara commanded them without hesitation after retrieving the Angel feathers.

In the blink of an eye, the road was clear. The only person left on it was Odara. She turned and walked towards the edge of the fortress that surrounded the Augustin home. Looking upward, she saw that the Sphinx was still sitting atop the protective light covering. Odara took to the air and landed next to the Sphinx. She bowed her head to it and then commanded the release of the protective covering. She and the Sphinx raised in flight at the same time as the covering began to retreat. The Sphinx traveled upward as Odara headed back to the ground in front of the Augustin house. Once the covering of light was completely gone, she stepped forward and embraced the wall of trees with her body. "I bid you, return to your natural state and thank you for your protection. Relinquish your hold on this estate."

She took a deep breath and blew a quarter-sized circle of fire into the wall of branches. The tree branches quivered and one by one started to release one another. It was an incredible sight. She watched intently as the intricately and tightly woven tree limbs receded. After all of the trees had separated from one another, the trees that appeared through multiplication started to retreat back into the earth. Odara was in awe of the forces at work. The elements and the earth itself assisting her was humbling.

When the last tree was gone, Odara turned her attention to the dome of fire that held the house and the Augustin women inside of it. She had to contain the fire to release the women. "Spread me out!" she yelled aloud. Odara opened her arms and began to duplicate herself. Shortly, there were fifty Odaras spread about, forming a circle around the fire barrier. All of them with their arms outstretched, moved in synchronicity as they stepped into the wall of fire and inhaled. The fire was swallowed by all of herself and all of the duplicates. Once it was completely gone, they each rejoined her body. Odara was standing adjacent to Intisar when the last duplicate entered her body. Intisar and her sisters were still bound by the thread of fire that connected them. Odara stuck her hand into the fire and said, "Cease!" The thread of fire dissipated and Odara passed out from exhaustion. The tin that held the salve from Amaterasu hit the ground the same time as she did.

Odara awakened a day later in the bedroom that she and Prentice had shared in the Augustin home. Prentice was in male form again and Lisa was gently applying the salve from Amaterasu to Odara's entire body. When her eyes opened, Lisa smiled at her. Continuing to massage her with the salve, Prentice asked her how she felt. "I feel fine. How do I look?" she responded. "Pretty good for someone who almost incinerated themselves." Prentice answered her and his eyes softened. The salve from Amaterasu was soothing and healing her body from damage caused by the intensity of the fire that she had used. Odara smiled at him and then a tear fell down her cheek. Prentice held her hand and said, "Before you grieve, I believe you should visit Intisar and Glenda." Odara turned her head away from him and responded, "I failed to complete my assignment. I'm sure the Sacred Council will be sending a message soon requesting my presence. I don't want to have to tell Intisar that I could not finish what I set out to do." Prentice leaned forward and kissed her on her forehead. "Go see them, they have something to tell and show you."

Odara fell back asleep while Prentice and Lisa were massaging the salve into her body. The next time she woke up, it was a few hours later, and the setting sun was filtering pink and yellow light through the curtains. Prentice, now back in the form of a cat, was sleeping next to her on a pillow in the bed. She sat up and started taking inventory of herself. She felt great, no aches, pains, or injuries that she could feel. The only thing that hurt was her heart. She was saddened by not finding out where the missing women were, but she knew she had to face Intisar. She wondered why Prentice had said Intisar *and* Glenda needed to see her.

Odara got out of the bed and dressed in the robe and slippers that were laid out on the chaise for her. She wrapped herself up tightly and left the room. She was going to see Intisar and deliver the news of her failure. As she headed down the hallway from the bedroom, she glanced at the walls again. This time, the mirrors were gone and in their place were paintings again. A series of beautiful paintings of bright lively flowers in full bloom. Some were on tables in vases and some were growing out of the ground. Every single painting had glorious images of flowers thriving. Odara thought, *that's nice*, and resumed her walk to the back house where the weavers worked.

Odara walked through the yard and entered the workshop. She was heading towards the room where Intisar worked and stopped when she heard an exquisite sound. Someone was in Intisar's room singing. Knowing that the sisters always worked alone in their individual spaces, she was surprised to hear a voice other than Intisar's from behind the door. Odara knocked and then opened the door. Intisar was seated at her loom. Glenda, the second eldest sister was standing beside her singing. Intisar's head was resting on Glenda's chest. Glenda was holding her sister as she sang, and Intisar's eyes were closed with a smile on her face. *Great,* Odara thought, *"I get to ruin a beautiful moment with my news*. She closed the door and both Intisar and Glenda turned and looked at her. Before she could speak, Intisar stood and almost ran to her.

Intisar took her hand and led her to the loom. "Look!" she exclaimed. Odara looked at the loom. Her eyes began to scan the tapestry that Intisar was working on. There were no holes! But that was impossible. She hadn't located the women. So what happened? Intisar told Odara that whatever happened caused her tapestry to self-mend and within hours, almost all of the holes were gone and the ones that were left were undetectable to the human eye. Odara said, "I don't understand." Intisar told her to run her hands across the tapestry and she would get the answers she needed.

Odara placed her hands on the tapestry and began to follow the pattern. What came to her made her scream aloud. The voices of the women that she thought she hadn't helped were speaking to her. Apparently, when the entity that she battled was destroyed, the spirits of the remaining missing women were released. They were all actively being physically rescued or released and were finding their way back to their lives. Some of them didn't want to go back to where they came from, but they were free. Free to continue living their lives and fulfilling their purposes.

Odara swooned and Glenda caught her by the shoulders. Glenda then spoke, "The children that I record have more than doubled in number and they are also safely returning to their families. One by one, they will all be where they belong. Glenda and Intisar wrapped their arms around Odara as she wept. She was drying her tears when the sound of tribal drums began to carry through the window on a breeze. She was about to tell them the time for her to leave had come when Ola and Linda, the twin sisters entered the room. In their arms, they both held tapestries.

Ola handed Odara a tapestry and she unfolded it to look at it. It was incredible. Ola had woven a tapestry with an image of Odara and Prentice in it. The likeness was that of a painted portrait and the color usage was incredible. Odara was dumbstruck and speechless. Linda stepped forward and opened the tapestry that she carried for Odara to see. Hit with the same reaction from viewing the first tapestry, Odara took a deep breath and exhaled. The tapestry that Linda held up had all of the sisters and Odara woven into it. They were holding hands in a circle, and there was a brightly colored Sun in the background. Odara was overcome with emotion. The twins didn't speak. They folded the tapestries and placed them in Odara's arms. Wrapping Odara up in a hug, they both whispered "Thank you" in her ears. Odara was outdone. She was still trying to process what Intisar had revealed to her. She turned to Intisar and Glenda, and Intisar interrupted her before she could speak. "We know. We hope you remember us and come visit one day for Sunday dinner." Odara responded with, "You can count on it." She held her tapestries up to her chest and walked past the twins out of the door.

When Odara returned to the bedroom, Prentice was sitting in the windowsill staring out into the yard of the home. The sound of the drums had started to increase in volume. Odara knew that it was time to return to the Chateau in the south of France. Saying goodbye to Prentice was going to hurt. She stared at him. He was sitting in the sill looking like a regular house cat. Never would she have imagined what she had experienced with him. She smiled at the thought of the power she felt when he entered her body to reinforce her strength for battle. She was taken by him, and she did not want to say goodbye. "Then don't," Prentice said without turning to look at her. She stepped towards him and Prentice assumed the form of the man he was while they were in San Francisco. This time, he wore white linen pants and a white linen shirt. He took her hand and said, "I hear the drums. That call isn't just for you. Our journey together isn't over.

Let's head to your Chateau. I've been many things but never a "*rich*" cat. They looked at each other and burst into laughter. "So be it,"

Odara replied. Prentice jumped into her arms back in the form of a cat and Odara threw her head back as she spoke, “South of France, to my Chateau, I have unfinished business there.” With a swirl of light and a gust of wind, they were transported through time and space to the dimension where Odara had originally been assigned. They landed in the courtyard in front of her home. Odara sat Prentice down and they walked towards the house together. Neither of them knowing that what was awaiting them inside of the Chateau, was another beginning of something incredible.

13
First Things First

Prentice stopped at the front door and looked back. The beauty of the courtyard in front of the Chateau was spellbinding. He looked up at Odara who was waiting patiently while he took it all in. "It's beyond beautiful, isn't it?" Odara asked. He responded with a smile in his eyes and then the front door opened. Giselle and Nicolette stepped aside to allow them to enter the place that Odara had just accepted as her temporary home before she was reassigned. "Welcome home, Mademoiselle." Giselle's voice was music to Odara's ears. She hadn't realized that she actually missed being in a place that she called home, even though she was only there for a brief period before leaving. "Thank you, Giselle. I'd like to introduce you both to…"

"Prentice!" Giselle and Nicolette responded at the same time. Instantly, Giselle reached down and picked Prentice up. He spread out across her chest like they were old friends. Odara looked at them, and before she could ask the question, Giselle responded, "We are very old friends." Prentice snuggled in Giselle's arms as she and

Nicolette stroked him and told him how much they had missed him. Odara was dumbfounded. She was about to continue with questions when the palm of her hand began to warm up. Nicolette looked at her and said, “You must be famished. I will have lunch ready in one hour. In the meantime, you have a guest in the drawing room.” Giselle stroked Prentice again and sat him down. “Yes, you have a guest in the drawing room. He has come every day since you left, and today, he came with something for you. Odara looked down at Prentice with question in her eyes and he smirked. “I’ve known Mutora and Roma for a long time, why are you surprised? You’re the youngest of this crew.” Odara stared at him and wondered who else he knew and where else has he been and how old was he really? “We’ll talk later. I want to see this magnificent home of yours and I’m dying to know who’s in that drawing room and with what for you.” Prentice turned and started walking towards the large double doors that were the entry to the drawing room. Odara shook her head and followed him.

Giselle opened the doors to the drawing room and Odara was pleasantly surprised to see Randall, the young artist who had painted her portrait, sitting in a chair by the fireplace having tea. As she was about to greet him, she looked up and saw the portrait he had painted hanging above the fireplace. It was exquisite. The colors, vibrancy, and accuracy were incredible. Her mouth dropped open. Prentice walked over to the fireplace and looked up at the picture, then looked back at Odara. "Magnificent" was the only word he could say. Randall stood up and greeted her. "Forgive me for coming unannounced, Mademoiselle Odara. I have been unable to rest ever since I brought you home and saw the beauty of your Chateau. I have something for you." Odara saw that there were four large wrapped packages up against the drawing room wall. As Randall walked over to them, the temperature in her palms began to rise again. She glanced over at Prentice whose tail was standing straight in the air. He was completely still, like he had just seen a mouse that he wanted to pounce on. Randall began speaking again. "After I last saw you, I was commissioned by an elderly gentleman to paint something for his collection of chateau paintings. He wanted different versions of a chateau, something interesting or intriguing, not just a chateau and its landscape. He paid me quite handsomely up front for two paintings and said that there were no time boundaries for their completion. I asked if there was a particular chateau he had in mind and the response was no, just one that hadn't been seen before. I immediately knew that your chateau was probably one that he wasn't familiar with, because no one I'd spoken with after painting your picture seemed to be familiar with your property. As a matter of fact, no one seemed to know that it had ever existed. It felt like… like your home just miraculously appeared out of nowhere. I know it sounds silly, but that made it even more absolute for me to use your home as the subject for his paintings. I cannot explain what you are about to see. All I can say is that I painted what I saw."

Randall began removing the wrapping paper from the packages as Odara and Prentice stood on edge, perfectly still like statues. As he was unwrapping each one, he leaned them up against the wall. When he was finished, he stepped back and exhaled. "I present to you Le Chateau Mystique." Odara was frozen where she stood.

Prentice walked over to her to be picked up. She swooped him up and stepped forward to look at each of the paintings. Randall had painted four pictures of her chateau. Every one of them was exact, down to the placement ofthe flowers in the courtyard and the details on the window frames. Then she noticed what set them apart from one another. In the first one, her silhouette was in the window looking out into the sky. The second one had a view of the back patio and a black cat… It was Prentice, sitting at the foot of the bench by the garden. Her body stiffened. *How could he have known about Prentice? Maybe it's just a cat.* "Look at the collar," Prentice said to her mind. Odara stepped closer to see the full details. The cat was wearing the jeweled collar that Giselle had given Odara before she left for her assignment. Odara couldn't take her eyes off the painting. Now she was perplexed. Prentice jumped down from her arms and walked over to the third and fourth paintings. "Odara, these next two will require some restraint from you. He has no idea what he has captured here." Prentices' message to her brought her back from her trance. Odara slowly walked over to the last two paintings. As her eyes began to focus in on them, she felt lightheaded and then a tinge of pain. Prentice assumed a male form and caught Odara before she hit the floor. Giselle entered the room swiftly and helped him move her to the chaise. Randall was quite alarmed and was about to ask if he could help when Nicolette appeared and blew something into his airspace. "Rest and forget," Nicolette said. Randall sank down in the large chair he had been sitting in when they first entered the room and was instantly in a deep sleep. Giselle began to tend to Odara who had fainted from the shock of what she saw in the last two paintings. Prentice stood and walked over to them with Nicolette. Understanding that Giselle and Nicolette were Odara's first family members, Mutora and Roma, two of the three people who were charged with bringing her first human form to life, Prentice was free to speak his mind. "She has been through a lot with her last two assignments. Maybe she's not ready. If the thought of it all knocked her out, how will she handle the next part of her journey? I will speak to the Sacred Council on her behalf if necessary. I want her to be ready, to be ready at all times for anything. She just fell out, and I sensed physical pain. She may be too connected to her humanness." Nicolette/Roma looked at the third painting. It was a view of the chateau from the orchard at sunset. Incredibly captured, the vibrance of the painting made you feel as if you could smell the fruit from the trees in the picture. Standing in the middle of the orchard barefoot, wearing a gold form fitting, heavily beaded gown and matching headpiece with full natural curls like a lion's mane underneath, was Odara—and she had wings. "No," Nicolette said, "she is ready. What makes her ready for the next level of her journey is exactly what you say makes her weak --- her humanness. It's what sets her apart from the other warriors. She feels and she cares. That part of her is just as important as the spirit warrior in her body. She needs them both to execute so fiercely." As Nicolette looked over the fourth painting, she heard Odara beginning to stir. The last painting was probably what had knocked Odara off of her feet. It was a view of the chateau from the road leading to the courtyard. Walking up the road in the picture was someone she probably thought she would never see again, definitely not in the body that she was occupying presently, and most certainly not in a time period other than the one she existed in – Older Odara.

Giselle was helping Odara to sit up straight and handed her a glass of water. Odara was slightly disoriented for a few moments and then she slowly began to get clear. She looked around at Giselle/Mutora, Nicolette/Roma, Prentice, and Randall, who was still knocked out asleep in the chair by the fireplace. As she gathered her strength, she stared across the room at the paintings and stood up on her own. "What is going on?" she asked. She felt… no, she knew that they knew something that she didn't, and she wanted to know what it was. "Someone tell me what is going on and who is Randall? How could he have painted what he painted? Why did I feel actual pain at the sight of my older self?

Someone answer me, please, before I get angry!"
Prentice took Odara's hand and tried to explain.
"Randall is just a very gifted artist. He knows nothing about you or who you are. Sometimes creatives are used to send messages or create maps through their work. He was telling the truth when he said he painted what he saw in his mind.

He's brilliant, talented, and headed for great success. Leave him out of your questions. As for the rest, all I can say is that we'll be hearing from the Sacred Council soon. The messenger is already preparing for his voyage to see you.

Then, and only then will your questions be answered. Unfortunately, we have not the authority to divulge anything further. All we can do is make sure that you are rested, cared for, and safe until the messenger arrives." Odara stared at Prentice. He was unmistakably beautiful whenever he transformed into human form. She began to soften as she glared at him. She wanted answers, and she knew that he would not betray his loyalty to his charge by giving them to her. So, all she knew was that Phillip was coming, sooner or later, and that she just had to wait.

"You make me sick, Prentice," she said aloud.
"So be it, love," Prentice responded and then reassumed his form as a black Persian cat. He snuggled up to her feet and she rolled her eyes. Giselle and Nicolette were definitely not going

to give up any further information either, gaging by the looks on their faces. Odara asked, "What's going on with Randall?" Nicolette giggled a little and responded, "He saw a bit too much. I'll awaken him, and he will pick up where he left off with no memory of anything other than you viewing the paintings before you passed out. Are you ready?" Odara looked at Giselle who had a look of "Get it together" on her face. "Yes, I'm ready," Odara replied.

Nicolette walked over to Randall and placed her hand over his eyes. "Musalateh, awaken now." Randall sat up in the chair, stood, and walked back to where he was standing near the paintings against the wall. He looked around and began to speak. "I hope that you are pleased. As I was saying… I was literally drawn to your chateau every day for almost three weeks. I felt like I wasn't in control of myself. I don't know where the images came from. I just knew that for some reason I had to include them. But here's the most interesting and puzzling part of it all: When I finished them, I went to the home of the gentleman who had commissioned me so that he could view them. When I knocked at the door, a young woman with children about her skirts answered the door. I asked for the gentleman and she said that no one by that name lived there or had ever lived there. I checked the address that I had been given by him and it was correct, but she was adamant that I had the wrong home. Of course, I was baffled but I didn't want to alarm her by insisting anything, so I just left. For days I kept an eye out for him at the part of the market where I sell my work, but I didn't see anyone even remotely like him. I even took the time to ask if anyone else had seen the gentleman that I'd had lunch within the open market, and no one remembered any of it. So, I decided that the paintings should go to you. I've already been paid. They are of your home, and no place is more worthy of their magnificence." Odara looked at Randall and could see that he was clearly puzzled. Prentice looked at her and giggled. "Never a dull moment with you, Mademoiselle Odara." She turned her back to Prentice and said, "Thank you, Randall, this is breathtaking work. I will have to think carefully of where to place each piece. You are on your way to being one of the greatest of our time, I'm sure of it." Randall smiled and kissed her hand.

"Very well then, I shall be on my way." Odara and Prentice walked him to the front door and escorted him into the courtyard. Randall turned to her and said, "It will be my pleasure to create for you at any time. Have a great day and thank you for receiving my gifts so graciously." "Absolutely, Randall, I'm sure I will be needing something for my boudoir soon. I know where to find you." Randall turned and began walking to his cart down the road. Odara was about to go back into the house and then she turned and called for him. "Randall, do you remember the name of the gentleman that commissioned you? I'm just curious." "Yes ma'am, yes I do. He said his name was Phillip." Odara stood blinking in disbelief as he walked away. She looked down at Prentice and he said, "Lunch should be ready by now, don't you think? And I am ready to tour the chateau. I can't wait to see what your initial assignment was, hopefully before it kicks in, we can have some fun. We are in definite need of some relaxation and some fun." Odara heard him but she was looking ahead into the sky. The sound of tribal drums was drifting to her ears through the wind. She couldn't imagine what was next, but after everything she had just gone through, she was ready. She was absolutely ready.

Contact Info

Instagram - carlajsart Facebook- facebook.com/carlajsart Twitter- isisthepoet

For more information including bookings and sponsorship opportunities:

www.carlajlawson.com

CPSIA information can be obtained
at www.ICGtesting.com
Printed in the USA
FSHW021003061020
74457FS